Puzzle Forest 1

The Secret City

James DuBern

Huspel

Chapter 1

"No more cackles!"

Norbert paced up and down the lounge, checking his watch every few seconds. On the table was his robot owl, with feathers made from orange guitar picks, and camera lenses for eyes. The unlikely child of a smart speaker and a salt shaker, Owly was Norbert's best and only friend.

"Right, do your grandma voice," Norbert said.

"Do I have to?" Owly whined. He watched a tennis match on a television, the salt crystals giving a slight crunch as his head rotated this way and that. "I'm the most advanced life form on the planet. I'm sure I can talk like a granny. Anyway, why can't the school just send a letter like normal?"

It had been over a year since Norbert's parents went missing. 430 days, to be exact, and he still twitched the curtains open at the slightest sound on the driveway. He had spent two birthdays and two Christmases without so much as a card or a hug, and he missed his mum and dad more than anything in the world. It was a tough time for a thirteen-year-old boy at a particularly terrifying school.

According to his teachers, Norbert remained safe in the care of his grandmother, but there was one problem with that story: Norbert didn't have any grandparents, only a robotic owl with an untested impression of one.

"This is the second parents' evening you've missed. They 'thought it would be nice' to speak to you in person," Norbert said.

"Whatever," said Owly, rolling his eyes. "I watched the Hansel and Gretel movie last night to get into character. It'll be fine."

"You did what?" Norbert asked in alarm. "Was that the only old woman you could find; a child-eating witch?"

Owly shrugged, his wings edging out from his body a touch. "If you had a real grandma, she could train my language model. It's not my fault."

"If I had a real grandma, I wouldn't need you to do this phone call," snapped Norbert. He was abuzz with nervous energy, ruffling his chestnut-coloured hair. "She could move in and make my packed lunch and play Scrabble and whatever else grandparents do when your parents go missing."

"I'm *amazing* at Scrabble," Owly said defensively. "And I may not be able to make your packed lunch but I did hack the school canteen and put thousands of dollars onto your lunch account."

Having the house to himself wasn't all computer hacking, late bedtimes and waffles for dinner. Norbert had to grow up fast and do all manner of parenty things, like figuring out the washing machine and how to unblock the toilet. (Don't ask.) Recently, he'd even battled his way through a bag of salad when Owly said he looked pale.

The phone rang and Norbert froze. He bared his teeth and looked at Owly, then gingerly picked up.

"Hello, it's Ms Denmark from school. Is that Norbert?"

"Yes, hello Ms Denmark," he answered, as calmly and politely as he could muster.

"Can I speak with your grandmother, please?" she said.

"Sure, I'll put you on speaker. She's right here," Norbert replied. He put the phone flat on the table between himself and Owly. The background noise of the busy school poured out through the phone's tinny speaker.

"Okay, can you hear me, Mrs....?"

"Mrs Graphite," Owly responded, in a voice that sounded like a broomstick-riding pantomime villain. Norbert's eyes widened in alarm.

"Mrs Graphite, was that? It's not a great line, I can't hear you very well," said Norbert's head of year.

"Yes, my lovely. Come closer so you can hear me. There's nothing to be afraid of," said Owly.

"Okay," said Ms Denmark, talking loudly into the phone. "I called to check that Norbert is in safe hands. He's doing very well at school."

"Yes, yes, my lovely. My house is warm, why don't you come inside?" said Owly. Norbert paced around the room, sucking through his teeth. He scribbled "Be normal!" on a scrap of paper. Owly shrugged helplessly.

"Norbert excels at the sciences, maths and computing. I'm sorry you couldn't be there to see him win the chess finals. One thing I wanted to mention; it would be great to see him put his hand up more."

"I'll boil him in my cauldron," Owly said firmly. Norbert let out a muffled shriek.

"I'm sorry, I misheard you," the teacher said.

"That boy is like my own children," Owly said.

"Ah. Mrs Graphite; I hope you don't mind me asking, but I understand you have difficulty leaving the house. Do you have plenty of food and everything you need to look after Norbert?"

Owly cackled gently, causing Norbert to bite his own fist to stop himself from whacking him.

"Yes, yes, my lovely. Plenty of sweets and cakes here in my house. Why don't you come inside? Nothing to fear here, my lovely."

Ms Denmark paused, clearly confused by this invitation.

"I won't be coming over to visit you, but thank you for the offer of, er, cakes and sweets. I just wanted to check that you were comfortable. There is support that can be provided, you know?"

"No, no. That won't be necessary. I will fatten him up here in my little cottage in the woods. Nothing to worry about, my lovely."

He ended the sentence with a chuckle that carried the squeal of a rusty gate. Norbert scrawled 'No More CACKLES!' on a cereal box and thrust it at Owly, who turned away dismissively.

"Well nice to speak with you Mrs Graphite, and Norbert. Are you still there?"

"Yes, I'm still here," he said, relief sweeping over him. "Everything is good. I will put my hand up more."

"Very well. And I notice sometimes you spend a long time in the bathrooms during lessons. Again, we ask that you use the toilet at break times."

"Yep, yep," Norbert said. "Will do."

"Okay. Have a good evening, both of you. And keep up the good work,

Norbert."

With that, the phone went silent and Norbert burst into a rant at Owly.

"Are you out of your mind? You're going to *fatten me up in a cottage in the woods*? All you had to say is 'yes' and 'no', not use all the dialogue from the movie!"

"Norbert, you worry too much," Owly said, returning his gaze to the tennis match. "My calculations showed that there was lower risk in using prebuilt sentences than if I chopped up the words and bolted them together."

Norbert slumped onto a chair, mentally exhausted by the call.

"The cackles!" he said, burying his face in a cushion.

"They were the best bits. Do you want to hear a recording?" Owly asked.

"No! Never," Norbert responded. "Well, maybe one day. What's the forecast like for tomorrow? Plane-flying weather?"

Owly rotated his head toward Norbert.

"It's perfect. I'll set my alarm for six, and we'll get it done before school."

Chapter 2

"Kill the engine."

N orbert shovelled down a bowl of oats and honey, spilling milk as he checked his watch.

"Are you sure we have time to get to the lake and back before school?" he asked.

"Yes," said Owly. "Hurry up and get the model finished."

Norbert slid his empty bowl into the dishwasher and retrieved a model aeroplane from a cupboard, manoeuvring it carefully to avoid the wingtips catching on the door frame. The replica passenger plane had a shining aluminium body, tacked together by rivets no bigger than the full stop at the end of this sentence. He set it onto a kitchen scale and called out the reading.

"Owly, this model weighs 268 grams. Can you work out how heavy each passenger should be?"

"That depends how heavy the real passenger was," Owly said.

Norbert looked sadly at his robot friend. He was barely able to force out the words.

"Mum is 67 kilos, dad is 80."

"For this model their correct weight is half a gram, give or take."

Norbert tore off a blob of plasticine, adding rice-sized slithers until it tipped the scale from zero to one gram. He split it into two sausages, one slightly fatter than the other, and fashioned each one into a Z shape so it could sit.

Inside the model plane were 25 rows of seats. He searched through a stack of papers until he found a letter from the airline. He scanned through it to find the information he needed.

"Seat 23C and 23D," he muttered. "Right at the back."

He set the models of his mother and father into their seats, the larger one by the aisle.

"Mum would have had the window seat. Dad would have insisted," he said.

Norbert reattached the roof of the plane and looked through the tiny window at his featureless parents, innocently awaiting take off. He pictured his mum deciding what movie to watch, and his dad looking up and down the aisle to see if the hosts were bringing out snacks. "If they offer you nuts, get some for me," he would have said. A tear rolled down Norbert's cheek and splashed onto the wing, wobbling the delicate model. He pulled his jumper over his thumb and wiped it off.

"Come on!" Owly said. "We have to get going if we're going to get this flown before school."

With Owly stuffed in his backpack and the plane in his hand, Norbert swung the front door open and stepped outside into a storm. He licked his fingertip to sense the wind direction and found his forearm blasted aside, arm-wrestled by the sky.

"Perfect conditions," he said, hopping down the steps and breaking into a run with his head down.

As he splashed along the pavement in the dawn light, he noticed a sleek black car pull alongside. The rear window slid down, revealing a smartly-dressed woman with pearl earrings and a beaming, if fake, smile.

"It's Norbert, isn't it?" the woman asked. "Do you need a ride to Blackstone High? We're heading that way."

"No, thank you," he called out.

She nodded and the car purred as it pulled away. Owly shouted from Norbert's backpack.

"Did someone just try to kidnap you?"

Norbert laughed. "Ha. Maybe?"

"You found some parents. Just the wrong ones," Owly quipped.

The surface of the lake was choppy, beaten into chaotic peaks by the gale. Norbert took out a tripod and drove the legs into the sand. He withdrew Owly from his backpack and stuck him on top, rotating him round and round to screw him down.

"This is humiliating," Owly complained.

Norbert shrugged. "I have to wrap you in cling film, too. You're not waterproof."

Owly's complaints were muffled as he was wrapped in plastic from his feet to below his eyes.

"Are you ready to record?" Norbert asked.

Owly made some incomprehensible noises, and Norbert tore a tiny hole around his beak to enable his friend to confirm. All the while, the wind tried to wrench the plane from Norbert's fingers and rain poured over the peak of his hood.

"Engage engine!" he called. The electrical motors whizzed into life and the propellers immediately became an invisible blur. "Remember Owly, it needs to fly at 67 kilometres per hour."

With that, Norbert hoisted the plane above his head and launched it like a javelin over the lake. The duo watched it ascend against the backdrop of slate grey thunderclouds.

"What's the altitude, Owly?" he bellowed over the thunderous wind.

"38 metres and climbing. 39. 40."

The model passenger jet was buffeted this way and that, several storeys above their heads. Norbert was distracted briefly by the thought of his parents inside, screaming for their lives. He pushed the frightful image from his mind.

"41....42 metres. It's there," Owly said.

"Kill the engine!" Norbert shouted.

The plane's propellers shut down and the metal model began to descend, gliding slowly at first but then hurtling towards the inky surface of the lake. Within seconds it careened into the turbulent water, exploded into parts and was swallowed in one inaudible gulp.

Chapter 3

"That ungrateful rat."

"Oh, it's the genius boy," Mrs Mansari said, leaning forward. "Driver, slow down please."

The car cruised behind Norbert, whose breath misted in the cold morning air.

"What's that in his hand?" Mr Mansari asked. He leaned across his wife to get a better view, catching her blouse with the gold stars and medals pinned to his military jacket.

"A model plane," she said. "He probably made it. He's a genius, you know."

A bang came from the boot of the car. Mr Mansari responded by thumping against the seat back.

They pulled up alongside Norbert, and Mrs Mansari lowered her window. When Norbert refused their offer of a lift, the driver picked up the pace and continued toward the school.

"That boy doesn't mind a bit of rain," Mr Mansari said, with fatherly pride. "Unlike SOME people."

Mrs Mansari looked down at her lap, her expression pained.

"Why do some people get that," she said, waving a hand at the pavement, "And we get that?" - this time gesturing over her shoulder.

Another thump came from the boot.

"Could you turn up the radio, driver?" Mrs Mansari said, massaging her temples.

Mr Mansari shook his head.

"I don't know what we did to deserve it. But at least we have the business."

Mrs Mansari smiled suddenly.

"Perhaps we could make a model plane? I bet that's the *in* thing. I'll have the design department mock something up."

The car pulled through the tall gates of Blackstone High. The schoolyard was empty and heavy wooden doors locked shut.

"Take it round back," Mr Mansari said. "Park up behind those bins."

He yanked his daughter's BMX from the bicycle rack on the back of the car, then popped open the boot. Dani, crawled out of it, dragging her school bag and blinking against the bright light and rain. Mr Mansari glowered at her in disgust, his voice all but a growl.

"When I say be by the door at 5:55am, I don't mean 5:59. I mean 5:55."

"Did she thank you for the lift?" Mrs Mansari asked when her husband returned to the car.

He shook his head as the vehicle turned towards the Mansari headquarters, where they would begin another day of making *'Toys That Delight!*

"Nope. I don't know what is wrong with that ungrateful rat."

Blackstone High was an imposing red brick school for the offspring of Carston City's elite. Brochures showed pupils in straw hats and blazers, holding lacrosse sticks and shiny trophies. Even the teachers drove nice cars, Dani thought, as she dragged her locker key along the side of one.

Between staff cars, Dani found a cardboard box and held it above her head up as a shield from the sleet. A fire escape door opened and she noticed a cook in a white apron and hat.

"You, girl," came a shout.

"What? I've done nothing," she said, stuffing her key in her pocket and stepping away from the scratched car. "It was like that when I saw it. Stop picking on me."

He looked confused.

"It's pouring. Come and wait inside," he said, holding the door to the kitchen open.

Dani paused for a moment before tossing aside her cardboard umbrella and stepping inside. She squeezed the water from her short black hair.

"You're awful early," the cook said, returning to his task of tidying the kitchen.

"The clever kids have to get here early," she mumbled. "There's a competition. Maths. Something about maths."

"Oh," he said. "You're a smart one, are ya?"

She shrugged.

He lit the stove and put the box of matches on a shelf. Dani had found a pack of hair nets and pulled one on over her wet hair. She took a box of blue plasters and put one on each ear, covering up ear piercings she didn't have. She looked at her reflection in a chrome fridge, casting her head this way and that.

He sniggered and cracked some eggs into a pan. "You wanna learn to cook?"

"Nah," she said, looking at her wrist where there was no watch. "I have to go. My special class is about to start. I'm the teacher, so I can't be late."

He nodded, and Dani slipped back out of the side door into the staff car park.

A few minutes later, the chef smelled burning, and darted around his kitchen to find the source of the smoke. His nose led him to the door, which he yanked open. Out in the staff car park, the dustbin containing cardboard was on fire.

Chapter 4

"There's a chance."

Norbert tossed his coat onto a radiator and rubbed his wet hair with a towel. He carefully dried off Owly, who ran a system self-checkup and confirmed that the water had not damaged his intricate circuitry.

"You must leave in the next eight minutes to avoid being late for school," Owly said.

"Yes, okay, *Grandma*," Norbert replied, his eyes fixed on the screen. "They expect everyone to be a little late when it's stormy like this."

He tapped at the keyboard, flicking through grey images so quickly they became a video.

"Look!" he said excitedly. Owly, who stood on the same table as the laptop, rotated his head 180 degrees so his cameras could watch the show.

On the screen were hundreds of photographs of the plane hitting the lake, all taken within the fraction of a second in which the impact occurred. What had looked to his human eye to be a single, instantaneous crash, now looked like a complex story with several chapters of destruction. The plane's nose crumpled as it smashed into the water, the wings torn clean off. Less than half a second after impact, the body of the plane cleaved in two, a crack racing around the aluminium like a bolt of lightning. The bulk of the aircraft disappeared below the surface, but the tailpiece of the rear section floated briefly. Norbert cycled the images forward and back until he isolated the single frame where the tailpiece was torn from the fuselage. He zoomed in on the jagged split and tapped wildly on the screen.

"Look, Owly! Count the windows from the back. As the plane sank, my parents would have been in the floating tailpiece. They could have swam out. I mean it's RIGHT there, look!"

Owly studied the image, narrowing his eyes as he processed an analysis of the impact.

"Norbert, my calculations suggest there's a nought point nought, nought..."

Norbert listened carefully, while he zoomed in until he could see the porthole his parents were sat behind. It was just a dark grey oval, but still he zoomed further until it filled the screen and maybe, just maybe he could make out their little plasticine heads.

Owly continued "...nought, nought, nought one percent chance that your parents could have survived that plane crash."

Norbert slammed shut the lid of the laptop and stared at him with wide eyes. "So you're saying there's a chance?"

"Go to school!" Owly replied, his head turning round and round.

"Wait!" Norbert said. "I haven't done my kung fu."

Norbert grabbed a couple of pencils and held them over the edge of the table.

"Imagine it's Dani's head!" Owly said.

Norbert swung his arm down with a 'hi-ya'. The pencils fell to the floor, unbroken. Norbert clasped his hand in pain and kicked them across the lounge.

"Aagh. I can't tell teachers about Dani because they'll want to chat with 'grandma'. My only hope is defeating her, but it's so hard! Owly, am I ever going to be a kung fu master? Be honest."

Owly rotated his head. "I calculate there's a nought point nought, nought..."

"Yeah, yeah," Norbert said dejectedly as he left the house.

Chapter 5

"You must be punished."

Norbert flip-flopped his father's watch on his wrist; too big even on the tightest setting. He stared at the second hand and wondered how many times per day it would form a right angle with the minute hand. He began to calculate it in his head, but found himself distracted by the graffiti on the wall. Among the incomprehensible etchings and nightmarish images were blood red letters bearing the unmistakable gloss of nail polish.

'Norbert if your reading this its too late'.

He swallowed, troubled immediately by two missing apostrophes. Not because he was a stickler for grammar, but because it bore the hallmarks of Dani. The boys toilets had long been his only safe refuge from her, but the dripping warning told him those days were over.

From inside his cubicle, he heard the main doors creak open. Norbert pulled his knees to his chest, propping his heels on the rim of the toilet seat where they would remain out of sight. The sole flapped away from the toe, as if even his shoes were gasping in fear. Norbert had meant to get new ones for months, but every evening he was consumed by the search for his missing parents.

He braced for a thump on his stall door, but instead heard a fellow pupil innocently wash their hands and then yank an unnecessary number of paper towels (seven!) from the dispenser.

The school toilets fell quiet once again, and Norbert, pulse racing, tried to calm himself with calculations involving the hands of his wrist watch. Ironically, trigonometry was the very lesson he was currently avoiding. But he dare not go back into that classroom because *she* would be there. His late nights working on the plane project had resulted in him forgetting a crucial piece of homework. Not his, of course; Norbert would finish maths worksheets before the teacher made it back to their desk. The homework he had forgotten was Dani's, which actually took him longer because he had to get some answers deliberately wrong, to avoid suspicion.

Fourteen minutes passed in a toilet cubicle which smelled of bleach (and worse), before the bell rang for lunch. A football game was the next dreadful event in his torturous day. Being a year younger than everyone in his class, Norbert was regularly picked as the ball itself. He would get kicked around the playground for an hour, before returning to lessons battered and bruised. But today turned out to be even worse.

As he washed his hands at the sink, the door swung open and in walked Dani and her sidekick, Marissa. This was the moment that Norbert had feared for the three years he had been at Blackstone High. His last safe refuge at school - the boys' toilet - had been invaded.

Dani, with blue plasters still on her ears, wore her hair scraped back for a fight. She casually chewed gum and seemed to delight in the juxtaposition of her calmness and Norbert's terror. She angled her head up to the ceiling and then hoiked her gum toward the terrified boy. The sticky pink blob bounced off his forehead before he had time to blink. The duo erupted into a hyena-like shrieks.

"So, thought you could hide away for half the lesson?" Dani said. "But if you're in here, whose work am I meant to be copying during the test? Didn't think of that did ya? Not so smart after all," she said, circling him and tapping his head.

Norbert backed away, his eyes trained on the sticky toilet floor.

"Shouldn't you be in the girl's toilet?" Norbert offered, meekly.

"Shouldn't *you*?" Dani spat in response.

Norbert backed up further and bumped into a metal waste-paper basket, causing him to stumble to the floor beneath a window. The thunderous storm rattled the glass. He thought of the plane hitting the lake, the jagged metal torn apart.

"I know kung fu," cried Norbert, summoning all his courage and putting his hands up like swords.

The girls glanced at each other and exploded into laughter. Dani closed in on him, her shoes burrowing through a sludge of wet paper towels. Norbert felt cold but sweaty at the same time, backed into a corner under a window. Dani rose up like a cobra, a flash of lightning reflecting on her ghostly skin.

"Remember Norbert, you work for me. When I say sit in front of me, I don't mean sit behind me. I don't mean hide in the toilets. I mean, sit in front of me."

"I'm sorry Dani, but..."

"No buts. You must be punished," she said, snapping her fingers.

Marissa strode over to Norbert, tightening her blond ponytail. She picked up the waste paper basket and slammed it down hard onto his head, where it stuck like a knight's helmet. The two girls high-fived and left Norbert dazed and broken on the bathroom floor.

Tears rolled down Norbert's cheeks, or maybe it was the soggy paper towels which blocked his vision. He couldn't tell anymore. He tried to extract the metal basket from his head, but the lattice squeezed so tightly against his ears that it wouldn't budge without inflicting more pain. He heard the bullies leave, then the sound a broom being slid into the door handle. He was trapped in the dank bathroom. Probably forever.

Norbert had naively stumbled into Blackstone High three years ago when his family moved to the city for his mother's job. She designed schools, hospitals and prisons, which she said were worryingly similar. Norbert had come home from his first day with a blazer sleeve missing and a pair of glasses drawn on his face. His parents reassured him that things would settle down, but two years later, life was worse than ever. Blackstone High was no place for a thirteen-year-old mathlete. Now he was stuck there, knowing that if he stopped attending, then the authorities would visit his house and realise he was living with only a robot owl for company. He limped towards the toilet door, unable to raise his right arm. He tried to call out for help but the bin muffled his cries. He headbutted the door to get the attention of an adult, but the clang was only met with uproarious laughter from the corridor beyond.

As Norbert stumbled around the bathroom, he wished he could skip the rest of school and be home with his little buddy, Owly. With the blocked doorway and the din of laughter coming from behind it, he knew the only way out was through the window. By tipping his head back and looking down over his cheeks, he saw a slither of green outside. The tops of trees, which shook in the wind.

Unable to pry the basket from his head, Norbert clambered onto a sink. With one foot jammed against a tap and the other wedged against a towel dispenser, he was able to reach across and unhook the window catch. It flung open and the shock of cold air toppled him onto the floor. The clatter silenced the bullies in the hallway. Norbert heard the broom being wriggled from the door handle, and knew there was only one escape route. As the toilet door burst open for the second time, he climbed back onto the sink and hauled himself into the open window frame, gripping the wall for dear life and summoning the courage to jump.

Chapter 6

"You'll never escape me."

Norbert cocked his head back and looked down at his battered black shoes, perched precariously on the sill. An icy wind blasted his fingers, gripping for dear life on a wooden window frame. Beneath him, a drop the height of a house. In front of him, the branches of a towering oak were within leaping distance. Maybe.

Across the room, the toilet door flung open. Through the metal mesh, Norbert could make out a mass of long black hair and a broom. Could this witch fly? There was only one way of finding out. Norbert flung himself toward the branch of the tree, crashing into the upper branches with open arms. The wet bark smacked his chin as he landed, denting the metal basket on his head. He grabbed desperately at leaves, twigs, anything - but they slipped against his fingers and he crashed down to branches below.

Through the bin on his head he could barely make out which way was up, and it barely mattered. Norbert smashed into the branches of the oak, his ribs taking impact like swings of a baseball bat. Wet leaves whipped against his body as he tumbled, and with a series of bruising thumps he cascaded through the tree and onto the grass below.

Norbert's vision flashed with purple. Dazed, and with great effort, he crawled onto his hands and knees and attempted to stand. He managed a few steps before collapsing in a dizzy heap. Above him, Dani burst into laughter from the window, and spat out into the sleet.

Norbert crawled towards the brick wall of the building, where he spotted a bicycle rack through the slit in his basket helmet. He smacked on the lip of the bin with the heel of his hand, and it came off his head, grazing his forehead. Lined up along the wall were bicycles. Black ones. Green ones. Mostly purple, flashing ones. Snowflakes were starting to settle, and through a pounding headache, Norbert located his well-maintained green racer. His was the bike with a missing saddle, which he knew for a fact was inside Marissa's locker. He fumbled in his pocket for a key, and undid the lock. As he did so, the doors to the school opened and Dani stood at the top of the steps, poking her head out into the snowfall.

"So you didn't die," she shouted. "Shame."

Norbert swung a leg over the crossbar, and went to sit down, yelping as he hit the empty seat post. He looked across at a black BMX, which was the only bike without a lock. Only Marissa and Dani herself could risk not locking it up.

"Nerdbert, you'll never escape me," Dani shouted, leaning against a stone pillar.

Black mascara ran down her cheeks into the crook of her wicked smile, like tears of a monster. Norbert kicked his bike away and grabbed Dani's BMX, watching her for a reaction. Her eyes widened in rage.

"Don't. Even. Think about it," she said, pushing away from the wall and pacing down the stone steps.

Norbert jumped onto her bike and kicked the right hand pedal up into position. He cranked down on it so hard that the back wheel skidded against the slushy ground. Dani gave chase, but Norbert was too fast, racing towards the school gates, the bike swinging beneath him. He could hear her platform shoes battering against the pavement. He clenched his eyes shut and stamped furiously on the pedals.

Dani's screams faded, and finally were lost in the noise of the wind and snow. As he swept through the school gates, he looked back to see her silhouetted against the cold bricks of Blackstone High. For the first time in ages, he felt a smile build on his face, and then adrenaline-fuelled laughter burst out of his chest.

Beyond the school grounds, Norbert approached a T-junction. He squeezed the brake levers but found they flopped limply against the grips. He dragged his tatty old school shoes against the tarmac and narrowly avoided a collision with a car. Heart pounding, he looked up the street in the direction of his house and then down at the black BMX he had stolen.

He lifted his hands from the pink rubber grips as if to check they were his own. Great flakes of snow melted as they hit his sweaty palms, red raw from gripping the bars with such vigour. What was he thinking, stealing the school bully's pride and joy? She would hunt him down at his house, he thought. She was probably after him right now on his own saddleless racer, so he set off again, down a gravel track which led into a deep, dark wood.

Under the the trees, the howl of the wind fell away, and Norbert could hear his heart thumping in his ears. He kept looking back, convinced that Dani was on his tail, as he surged deeper into the dark forest.

After countless turns, Norbert rolled to a stop, exhausted. He had no idea how long he had cycled, or where he was. Through the canopy, the sky looked even darker than before. The leaves had lost all sense of green and were now just black silhouettes against the bruised, inky sky. He listened for signs of life, but heard only the call of a wood pigeon and the whistling wind beyond the treetops.

Norbert thought of Owly, and how easily he could have found a map and plotted a route out of the woods.

He picked up Dani's BMX and began to pedal back up the path in the direction from which he'd come. At every juncture, he tried to remember a waymarker, but the endless forest gave no clues. Frozen streams, fallen silver birches, jagged logs. He could be anywhere. Within half an hour, the light was so low that he could barely see the path in front of his wheel. Mud splattered up his legs, and he wished he had his proper bike with its sensible mudguards and lights. Even without a saddle it was better than Dani's ridiculous BMX, which didn't even have brakes. The snow was settling now, and Norbert was well and truly lost.

In the midst of telling himself off, he began to pick up speed on a long curling descent down a slippery trail. Unable to brake, he tried to drag his feet on the floor, but they just slid against the slush. Suddenly he hit a log across his path and was catapulted over the handlebars. He screamed as he swam through the air, hurtling off the path and into a steep ravine. His shoulder was the first body part to hit the ground and he rolled down the muddy hillside like a ball. His thighs and ribs battered into tree stumps as he tumbled like a pinball, down and down.

And then, black.

Chapter 7

"Danger of death."

Baz picked the moss from a rusted metal padlock, squinting through the rain. The torch clenched between his teeth cast a beam through the predawn darkness and his fingertips turned white with effort as he grappled with the stubborn, rain-slicked lock. A wrinkled poster fluttered against the brick wall as the demolition worker open the gates with a squeal of aged metal.

"DANGER OF DEATH. Keep out. By order of the Hawks."

Baz climbed back into his truck and slid the heat to maximum. While he waited for the windscreen to clear, he flipped down the sun visor and looked in the mirror. He squeezed his jaw, and reddish grime from the padlock smeared across his cocoa skin like war paint. Next to him, a red-headed girl of fourteen tried to sleep.

"Don't mess this up," he whispered, giving himself as stern a look as the gentle giant could muster.

"I bet you mess it up," the girl said, eyes still closed.

The truck crawled up a gravel driveway until its headlights splashed onto the white columns of a building. Baz leaned forward until his cheek felt the cold of the windscreen. He stared up at the building. It was more cathedral than house, with ornately carved gargoyles perched around arched windows.

"Nuts, wake up. Look at this place!" he said.

"We're knocking *this* down?" she said, craning her neck to take in the multiple storeys and stone chimneys "Whoa. Go–to–work–day just got fun!"

He reached across her and thumped down the door lock.

"*I* am knocking this down. You agreed, Nuts. You wait in the car and watch."

She nodded, already distracted by a screwdriver she found in the truck's door pocket. Baz reached over and took it from her, barely taking his eyes off the paperwork he was studying. A pink form had the word CONFIDENTIAL stamped so firmly that he felt the indentation before he read it. The address was correct and he confirmed the date on his watch.

"I mean it, Nuts. This is a really important job. I can't mess this up."

"Don't worry, Baz. I'm only here for this stupid school project. Don't think I *wanted* to get up at five in the morning and watch you beat up a building. What time's breakfast, by the way? Your job has breakfast, right?"

Baz got out and grabbed the sledgehammer from the bed of his pickup truck. One carefully placed hit against the front door caused a spark, and the black metal lock shattered. Inside, Baz was immediately hit by the smell of musty decay. With only a small circle of torchlight, he examined the hallway one item at a time. An ornate blue vase holding a single umbrella. It was like nothing he had seen before. Not since he was a kid, anyway. A chandelier that sparkled back at him. Finally, an enormous bank of light switches.

He flicked them all on and suddenly felt swamped by the cavernous manor house. To his left was a library, stacked to the ceiling with books. To the right, a lounge with a grand piano, a tattered armchair and a fireplace big enough to park a car inside. On the walls hung grand paintings of men and women wearing monocles and serious expressions.

A grandfather clock sat stopped, frozen in time like the rest of the house. With only a few hours until sunrise, he hurried to the telephone in the hallway and dialled a number.

"What?" came a groggy, female voice.

"Sonita, it's Baz."

Silence hung in the air.

"It's six in the morning," she groaned.

"I know. I'm sorry. I'm at this building. I need to check I had the right address. The manor house on the top of the hill, right?"

"Yes," she said. "You have the paperwork, don't you?"

"I do. It just doesn't make sense. The place is incredible. I've never seen anything like it. Paintings. Books. Stonework from the old era. Surely it doesn't need flattening?"

The line went quiet and Baz held the receiver away from his ear, brushing dust from the black plastic. His breath misted in the night air. "Hello? Are you still there?"

After an impatient exhalation, Sonita responded.

"Baz, just follow the orders. You know not to ask questions."

"Sonita, this is a three, four person job. You want me to level a house on my own?" he pleaded.

"That's why you're there at 5am, Barry. I was told to put one person on it, in the interest of confidentiality."

"Oh. And you chose me?" he said, flexing his shoulders back a little. Sonita sighed.

"Cassie broke her ankle kicking in a door. Pete is on his last warning for smashing up the wrong house. So I 'chose' you. Remember; slow and steady, careful deconstruction. This job was booked by the executives. They want it kept quiet. You mess this up, Baz, and.....well. You know."

The line went dead.

"I do know," he said under his breath. Baz yanked on a string that tightened his hood around his face, leaving only his eyes and mouth exposed to the cold night. The ramps on the back of his trailer crunched onto the gravel driveway and he backed his battered yellow digger onto the battlefield. He glanced back at the truck to check that Nuts was still in place, and she gave a thumbs up. Through a grimy windscreen he took one last look at the beautiful building and shook his head with the shame of what he had to do.

With a mighty swing, he smashed the bucket into the upper level of the house. A window exploded inwards, glass showering the carpet of a bedroom.

"Yeah Baz!" Nuts shouted from the truck.

The roof sagged down and a gutter swung free, denting the roof of Baz's digger enough to knock his ear defenders over his eyes. He grasped at a lever but had already committed to another pulverising blow. The long arm of his excavator crashed through a brick wall and re-emerged with a four-poster bed entangled in the scoop. A crack appeared between two rows of bricks, then splintered across the facade of the building.

"Nooo," he shouted, pulling the ear defenders off his face and flinging them out of the window.

Baz watched helplessly as the entire front wall peeled away from the building like a tsunami of brick. Before he could escape, the wave broke, dumping rubble over the arm of his vehicle. As his cab was see-sawed into the air, Baz stamped on the pedal to escape, but the avalanche of bricks and glass had him trapped. Through the smashed opening where a windscreen used to be, he watched the roof of the building keel over towards him. Roof tiles launched into the front garden, stabbing into the wet, mud-like gravestones. Baz dived out of the vehicle into a bush and watched in horror as the demolition took on a life of its own.

Nuts watched the chaos from the safety of the truck, her jaw hanging open.

With the brickwork gone, the skeleton of the building was now exposed, twisting and bowing under the weight of debris. Great wooden beams snapped like toothpicks and furniture rained down from the upper level. So deafening was the cacophony of destruction that when the grand piano was crushed, Baz didn't hear a note. A great stone staircase fell like an oak, sending a domino rally of stone pillars that crushed what was left of the yellow digger. Finally, the carnage subsided and the building looked like it had been hit by a meteor.

Baz waved away thick grey dust and pulled back his cuff to check the time. The entire demolition had taken three minutes.

"Ooops," he said, his teeth crunching on building dust as he moved his jaw.

He edged toward the ruins, waving away smoke. Broken pipes stuck out of half-fallen walls. Ice cold water sprayed angrily in every direction, fighting against the driving rain. The remains of the building had settled in mountains of rubble, and as Baz walked over them, they moved beneath his boots like a monster giving its dying breath.

In the collapsed heart of the building, he recognised a yellow sofa, buried under broken glass and criss-crossed by roof beams. He put his hands over his ears to stop the incessant ringing, but it only seemed to get louder with every step. He stepped onto the front door, which slid like a surfboard atop a stubborn piece of furniture and dumped Baz onto the hallway floor. Only then did he see the telephone, which had somehow survived, and was ringing. He crawled toward it and lifted the receiver to his ear.

"Finally!" came Sonita's voice. "Glad I caught you before you start. Don't forget to turn off the electrics and the water supply. Sorry if I was grumpy earlier. I'm not good at mornings."

He attempted to reply but his mouth was so thick with dust that only a puff of smoke came out. He hung up on his boss and looked around nervously. Everywhere he looked, he saw cables. Red ones. Green ones. Ominous yellow and black striped ones. All of them baring fork-like copper tongues that sparkled and crackled in the darkness.

He stood up and backed away from the hissing, menacing wreckage. As he stepped over mountains of books in what used to be the library, the floor broke beneath his feet. He fell through the ground and as he did so, his instinct was to reach out and grab something. Anything. But that thing turned out to be an electrical cable, as thick as rope. Baz clung onto the wire, suspended in the darkness below the ground. He aimed his headlamp into the subterranean chasm beneath his feet, and the spot of light reflected on a soup of black water peppered with floating books. Baz gripped the cable with white fingers, electricity crackling from its tip below his feet. He tried to climb but it was too slippery.

"Nuts!" he shouted.

The rain continued to hurl down, rushing over the jagged concrete piles and emptying into the basement in waterfalls. If the water level rises, he thought, it will meet the sparking electrical cable. He scrambled against the plastic red cable once more but only slipped further down.

"Nuts! Help!" he shouted.

The teenager finally appeared at the top of the hole, looking down at him.

"Nuts, you have to find the electrical box," he said, filled with relief. "It will be in the garage."

She looked around at the bombsite Baz had created.

"What garage?" she asked. "Shouldn't you have turned the electrics off first?"

"I know, I know. Just go look over there," he said with a nod. "Find the big red switch and turn it off."

Nuts clambered over the mountains of rubble until she found what looked like a garage door, crumpled like tin foil. Among the debris she spotted a thick black cable and followed it, throwing bricks aside to unearth a box.

"There are two red switches," she called over her shoulder in Baz's direction. "One is up, one is down. Does up mean on or off?"

She listened for Baz's response but could only hear rain.

"Eenie, meanie, minie, moe," she said, bobbing her head this way and that.

Meanwhile, Baz felt something under his foot, and looked down to see a steel box floating in the dank water. It was huge, like a refrigerator or a storage crate. He tried to stand on it, but it submerged under his weight. Suddenly the exposed wires at the torn end of the cable brushed against the steel face of the box.

Nuts, who figured it was 50:50, flicked the right hand switch down.

BOOM!

Like a lifetime of firework displays compressed into one tiny moment, a shower of sparks exploded out of the basement. Baz clutched the cable and squeezed himself into a ball, fortunately hanging above the water.

No sooner had it arrived than it was gone. The fizzing snake was dead, and once again the basement was dark, but for the beam of light from Baz's head torch.

"Okay, down is on," Nuts shouted, staring at Baz and his frazzled black hair. "I know for next time."

Stunned that he was still alive, Baz's eyes readjusted, and eventually he could make out the box floating in the basement was now open. Something was moving inside. He blinked, but all he could see was a black blob inside a pool of white light.

As his brain came back online, Baz realised that the electrical explosion had tripped the fuse and shut down the power. He timidly dangled a toe into the water, and when he found it was safe, he dropped into it. Freezing, black water soaked him to his waist. He waded to the box and shone his light into it. There, floating among splinters of wood and leather bound books, was a person. A fully dressed boy, in what looked like a blazer, black trousers and leather shoes with the soles flapping away at the toe. Baz adjusted his torch to get a better look at his discovery. And through deep blue eyes, the boy blinked back at him.

Chapter 8

"I found a fox."

A phone rang, waking Norbert up in a state of confusion for the second time that day. He tried to make sense of his surroundings as the phone rang incessantly, seeming to get louder as he shivered, clutching at the blankets that cocooned his body, trying to shake off the memory of ice-cold water.

Colourful sheets of fabric hung on the walls, leading up to a point in the tall ceiling in the middle, almost like a circus tent. He was on a sofa that sagged in the middle, and aside from the theatrical flourish, the room was a bland affair, with a vintage television, plain white walls and a telephone which rang, and rang, and rang.

A tall man with rich, walnut-coloured skin darted in and picked up the phone. Norbert hauled himself into a seated position, rubbing the heels of his hands onto his eyes.

"Thanks for calling back," Baz said. He covered the receiver and mouthed the word *police*, for Norbert's benefit. The boy's eyes widened and he shook his head violently. He tried to say 'stop' but his mouth was as dry as cotton, and barely a squeak came out.

"I was working at a demolition site earlier today," Baz continued. "I found…"

Norbert threw back the blanket and stumbled to his feet. His legs immediately buckled and he crashed to the living room floor. He began to pull himself toward Baz with his hands.

"Aagh! I found…" Baz continued, backing away in horror as Norbert swam across the rug toward the telephone. As the man mumbled and stuttered, Norbert's arm shot out and wrenched the plug from the wall.

Baz hung the receiver back onto its hook, and stooped to plug it back in. Norbert staggered back to the sofa, yanked the blanket over his shoulders and buried his face in a cushion.

"Sorry," he said, his voice muffled. "No police. I don't want to be found."

Baz sat on the coffee table and sighed, eventually coaxing the cushion out of Norbert's grip and making eye contact with the boy.

"Your parents must be worried sick. I was on the phone to the Hawks. They can get you home."

The construction worker saw him struggling to talk and fetched a mug of water. Norbert guzzled it down, and then another. His entire body felt dry, from his throat to the skin on his forearms.

The phone rang, once again.

"I have to get this. Look, kids run away from home all the time. You're not the first. Your parents won't be mad at you. We have to get you home."

Baz stepped toward the phone.

"My parents aren't at home. They went away," Norbert explained. He stood up, holding onto the back of the sofa to steady himself. The ringing continued.

"Who do you live with, then?" Baz asked, hand hovering over the phone.

"They're missing, but they're coming back. Please, I'll get out of here and find my house. Just don't get the police involved," Norbert pleaded.

The shrill ringing seemed to grow louder and louder in the silence between them.

"Trust me. This is what has to be done," Baz said. "I'm sure the police will be able to help."

"I don't need their help! I've avoided the police for a year and everything's fine. Just hang up and let me go," Norbert said.

Baz snatched the receiver from its dock, and exhaled. He slowly brought it to his ear, and cleared his throat.

"Sorry, I don't know what happened," he said. "The connection dropped."

Norbert listened intently, but could not make out the operator's words. With wide, desperate eyes, he stared at Baz, who turned to face the wall to avoid the panicked stare.

"Yes, that's right. As I was saying, I was at a demolition site, and..."

He breathed in slowly.

"I found...yes. I found a fox."

A pause hung in the air. Norbert raised his eyebrows.

"I wasn't sure whether to report it. I haven't seen one in a long time. I didn't know if they were a controlled species. Are they dangerous?"

Baz placed the phone handset back in its cradle.

"They hung up," he said. "I'm Baz, by the way."

"I'm Norbert."

Norbert listened to the clatter of china mugs set onto a worktop. The hollow, metallic rumble of water filling a kettle. The click, click, click of a gas stove being lit. With so much confusion in his mind, it felt good to close his eyes and understand something.

"How do you take your tea?" Baz called from the kitchen.

Norbert wasn't sure what the question meant. He could picture steam rising from a murky brown liquid, but couldn't remember if he had ever tasted it. How do you *take* tea? Eager to be a grateful and unfussy guest, he decided to plump with the image in his mind.

"In a cup with a handle, please," he called back.

His response was met with a deep chuckle, and Baz returned a few moments later with two mugs of tea, both with handles. He drew back the curtains, shocking the room with daylight. Norbert stood up, pausing for a moment to let the feeling of light-headedness pass.

"May I?" Norbert asked, motioning toward the window.

Baz shrugged.

His gaze was met with towering buildings, bursting with foliage. Hulking grey concrete blocks jutted into the sky, like jagged cubes stacked by a giant. The grubby grey boxes were peppered with windows like the one he stared through. Even with his forehead resting on the cold glass, he could not make out the ground below, only a blur of grey and green. Plants wrapped around the tower blocks and trees sprung from platforms in the sky, as if a slow motion dance was taking place between society and nature.

"Where are we?" he asked, gripping the window sill tightly.

"28589," Baz replied. Norbert looked at him blankly, so he continued. "Tower 28. Fifty-eighth floor. Flat 9. Which block do you live in?"

Norbert shook his head and stepped away from the window. He moved unsteadily and Baz reached a strong hand beneath his shoulder to help the boy sit back down.

"I don't live in a block. I live on Sandwell Street. Why am I here?" Norbert asked.

"That's the question," Baz said. "Early this morning I found you in the basement of a building I was tearing down. Do you remember that? There was an electrical explosion, and then I found you in a flooded basement. It was a miracle. A few more minutes and we would have... Well, don't bear thinking about." Baz shuddered. "What were you doing down there? Playing hide and seek? Did you break into that house?"

"I don't know," Norbert confessed. He sipped the tea and singed his lips. "All I know is I woke up and my ears were ringing and it smelled of burned hair. My eyes felt like they were shut when they were open. I was in a box or something, like a boat or a fridge. Soaked. Then I suppose you picked me up and now I'm here."

Norbert inspected his baggy pair of trousers, so long that only his toes poked out of the end of the leg. He wore a belt that had an extra hole drilled into it, a great distance from the others. His shirt swamped him, even with both sleeves rolled up.

"When you found me, was I...naked?" he asked.

Baz shook his head.

"No, you were in a school uniform, I think. But it was soaked so I put you in new clothes. Hope you don't mind. You fell asleep in the car, and we couldn't get any sense out of you."

"We?" Norbert asked.

"I was with Nuts. She's a friend's daughter, who came to work with me today. Norbert, what's the last thing you remember before the box?"

Norbert squinted as he tried to sort through his hazy memories. "I was at school. There was a fight in the toilets. I was going to do kung fu but instead I jumped out of a window. Then I borrowed a bike and I was cycling, and then...I think I crashed. It was snowing."

Baz ran a finger along a calendar on his wall. November had a photograph of a woman with a shock of curly blond hair, sitting on a sledge pulled by a herd of domestic cats. In December she was in a mechanic's suit pretending to work on the engine of a snowmobile. In January, she was curled up among puppies.

Baz scratched his head.

"I don't think it has snowed since Thursday or Friday, so I reckon you've been down there a day or two. Where were you cycling to?"

Norbert screwed up his face, trying desperately to follow a train of thought.

"Home, I think, but I got lost. Perhaps I crashed into the building site and fell down the hole. How far are we from Sandwell Street? Or Blackstone High?"

Baz rested a sympathetic hand on Norbert 's shoulder.

"I haven't heard of them, but they must be around here somewhere. So, you say your parents are missing?"

Norbert 's face turned the same colour as the building dust speckled in his messy brown hair.

"What's up buddy?" Baz asked.

"My parents are...away. Not forever. They're alive. I'm sure of it."

Norbert's face brightened as he recalled the plane test. "Last week, me and Owly figured out that they could have survived the crash. I just have to get home now and work out where. There are islands throughout the sea. Maybe they're on one."

Baz gave him a suspicious look.

"Owly?"

"My robot owl. He's not really a robot. He's alive."

"Yeah, I used to have one of those," Baz said, wistfully. "Course, we don't have them anymore."

Norbert looked surprised.

"You had a robot owl? That could talk and stuff?" he said.

"Of course, everyone did when they were your age."

Norbert narrowed his eyes, but didn't question his host. Baz scratched his head, looking out of the window for a solution.

"Norbert, if I let you stay here and don't report you to the Hawks, then I'm going to get done for kidnap."

"What's a Hawk?" he asked.

"Police. You haven't heard of the Hawks? Norbert, you might have hit your head when you crashed. We really should take you to a doctor."

"I'm fine, Baz. Sorry, I do remember the Hawks, of course. Everything's good. Baz, do you have some shoes I could borrow? I will leave right now, find my house, then bring them back. I don't want to be any trouble."

Baz slumped into an armchair and sighed.

"Because you did such a great job looking after yourself last time," he said. "No. You're staying here, where I can keep an eye on you. I've got a mate, Kara, who will know what to do. We have to search the missing persons register. Then you'll see that your parents are missing you."

"And you won't call the Hawks?" Norbert said.

Baz exhaled slowly. "Not yet."

Chapter 9

"Bring the map!"

Baz crouched by Norbert's feet and yanked a pair of laces, pulling the boot leather as tight as it would go.

"How's that?"

Norbert took a few steps, the heavy boots slapping on the beige carpet. "Great," he said.

Baz furrowed his brow.

"Be honest Norbert," he said. "You don't have to lie to me."

Norbert gently nibbled on the inside of his cheek. "Ok. It feels like I've inserted each foot into the sun roof of a car."

Baz chuckled, and slapped Norbert warmly on the back. "That's better, lad."

He crouched, his tone becoming more serious. "Now listen, we're going out to see Kara. If anybody talks to us on the way over, don't say a word. I'll deal with them. Okay?"

Norbert nodded, and followed Baz out of the flat and into the cold evening. The two of them set off down a walkway, and Norbert's stomach lurched when he glanced over the balustrade and saw the terrifying drop to the ground below. He swapped sides so he could hug the inside wall along the building, passing the front doors of Baz's neighbours. The lift took some time to arrive, during which time Baz looked anxiously up and down the gangway. When the doors finally opened, it was empty. Baz breathed a sigh of relief.

On the fourteenth floor, they took a footbridge which linked Baz's tower block with one across the street. Dim lights gave the skyway a greenish glow, and the wind blew a paper bag along in front of them. Through a metal grid, Norbert paused to take in the street below. It was completely devoid of cars, with just a few pedestrians making their way home with their heads down. Beyond the tower blocks was a sea of streets that disappeared into the mist. The sheer number of trees made it unlike any suburb he had ever seen. He jogged to catch up with Baz.

"The house you found me in. Are you sure it wasn't in Westover Street? Could it have been my house?" Norbert asked.

Baz chuckled, flipping up his hood so he could better hear him over the whistling wind.

"No, it wasn't your house. Unless you're Trixie's kid, you ain't got a house like that."

"How so?" Norbert asked, determined not to ask who Trixie was.

"Look," Baz said. "All the buildings in the city are concrete. Whether you live in the towers or the streets, your house is a grey block. It'll have walls and keep the rain out, just, but it ain't winning a beauty contest. But this one was stunning. It was made of bricks and wood, and had columns around the door like a palace in a fairy tale."

"So, why did you knock it down?" Norbert pondered.

Baz raised his hands like a caught bank robber. "I double-checked, and they definitely wanted it flattened. It broke my heart, but I do what I'm told."

He rang the doorbell on flat 54134 and an arm shot out as it opened, yanking him inside. Norbert darted in behind Baz, before he too was assaulted.

"Did anyone see you arrive?" a woman asked anxiously, closing the door and double-locking it behind them.

Baz calmly took his coat off and hung it on a hook in the hallway. "No. Nice to see you, too, Kara. Thanks for inviting us over."

She followed her guests into the living room, fussing with her floral dress. Norbert noticed a girl flopped over the back of the sofa, her spine arched in a way that made him wince. Her red hair hung down to the floor.

"Nuts!" Kara said. "We have visitors."

The girl rolled her eyes and let herself slump to the floor, where she remained in a heap of denim.

"You remember Nuts?" Kara asked Norbert, who shook his head.

"Well, that's my daughter, Nuts. All I can do is apologise. Come through."

Norbert followed Baz into the kitchen, where a dining table was set for four. The walls had mustard colour tiles and the floor had a plasticky linoleum that undulated slightly. The smell of pastry came from the oven, and Norbert realised he was desperately hungry.

Kara looked at him appraisingly, reaching across to put the back of her hand on his forehead.

"Hello. Can you hear me?" Kara said, slowly and loudly, pausing between words. Norbert and Baz looked at each other.

"He's not deaf! He's lost his memory," Baz chuckled.

"Have I?" Norbert asked.

"Oh okay, let's all laugh at silly old Kara!" she said. "How are you feeling, love? What can you remember?"

Norbert shrank against the attention. Even Nuts was watching him from the lounge, with her big blue eyes.

"I don't recognise these buildings," he said. "I don't think I've seen a tower block with so many trees. I live on Westover Street. Can we look it up?"

"Nuts! Bring the map," Kara called to her daughter.

A few minutes later it was slapped onto the dining table. Kara thumbed through the index.

"It goes Westland Street, then Wington Place. There's no Westover Street," she said.

"24 Westover Street, Carston City," Norbert added, a note of desperation in his voice.

The three of them looked at each other blankly, then back at Norbert. "This is Puzzle Forest," Nuts told him. "I've never heard of Carston City."

"Can't you look it up on the computer?" Norbert asked the adults. "Or your phone?"

"We don't use computers anymore," Kara said quickly. "And the phone..." she gestured to the wall, where her phone was mounted at shoulder height. A green, banana shaped part was connected to a main unit with a coiled cable. It had no screen, and only a ring of numbers which, Norbert presumed, were operated by dragging them with a finger. It looked like a relic from a museum. Beside it hung the same calendar he had seen in Baz's apartment. The blonde woman's fixed smile seemed even wider in the kitchen light.

"We'll find it," Kara said warmly. "Don't worry."

Nuts sat down and dropped her forehead onto her placemat. Copper-coloured hair flooded the plastic tablecloth and poured over its edge.

"Nuts, what did we talk about?" Kara said, sweeping hair from her guests' placemats.

A muffled answer could not disguise the sharpness of the words.

"We talked about basement boy coming over so I can't watch Billy the Carrot."

"What's Billy the Carrot?" Norbert asked, without thinking.

Nuts rose up, dragon-like, a fire in her eyes so raging that Norbert backed away until his shoulder blades hung over the back of his chair.

"You don't know Billy the Carrot?" she hissed.

He shook his head.

"Nuts, why don't you and Norbert play in your room. You can tell him all about Billy," Kara prompted.

Nuts rolled her eyes so hard that it took her whole body with them. She peeled off her chair, sliding onto the kitchen floor in a tangle of limbs. Like some sort of other-worldly insect, she crawled down the hallway and into her bedroom.

Norbert looked at Kara, who smiled and gestured for him to follow.

Chapter 10

"A carrot with legs."

N uts' carpet was thick with junk, which she made no effort to sweep aside before sitting down. Norbert hovered in the doorway, unable to see even a single boot-sized enclave in which he could place a foot without crushing something.

He looked at the posters, plastered at haphazard angles that triggered an urge to straighten them out. It seemed her interests included rock music, motorcycle daredevilry and, oddly, a huge radio antenna.

"Shut the door," Nuts ordered.

The rumpled duvet featured a human-sized carrot, grinning eagerly back at them. A light bulb hung from the ceiling, entombed in purple sweet wrappers. It gave the room the haunting glow of a witch's cavern.

Norbert sat cross-legged with his back to the door, holding a toy soldier which he had moved to make room. The plastic figure of a woman was naked except for wings; leaves taped between her outstretched arms and torso. Norbert reached across to place it on a bookshelf and Nuts darted towards him and smashed it from his hand.

"It doesn't go there!" she said, her face so close he could smell a combination of sweets and barbecue crisps on her breath.

The doll lay face down on the carpet, crash landed next to an odd sock and a toilet roll with the words 'Actual dinamite' misspelt in red marker. Nuts returned to her position at the other side of the room.

"So you want to know about Billy the Carrot?" she sighed.

Norbert looked at the duvet cover, and a poster of Billy in which he held a frying pan over his shoulder.

"Err. It's okay. I think I get it," he said.

"Oh, you're an expert now?" she recoiled.

"He's a character, I assume? A carrot with legs."

Nuts screwed her face up so hard that when she finally released the tension, it was like a firework detonating in the dark room.

"What are you *talking* about?" she said. "A carrot with legs? You come in here without knowing nuffing about BTC and suddenly you're an expert?"

"No, I don't mean that, Nuts. I just don't want to impose. You seem like you didn't want visitors tonight."

"I didn't. Because if you knew anything, you would know Billy the Carrot is on tonight. But no. We can't watch TV tonight, because Baz dug up a naked goblin in a basement and he's apparently SO important that we can't watch television. Ever again. Like, we literally have to DIE of boredom because..."

Her tirade was cut short when the bedroom door squeaked open. Kara poked her head in and smiled.

"Aw, look at you two! Lovely. Sausage rolls are almost ready."

The waft of home-cooked food made Norbert's mouth water. He felt a sense of dread when the door closed again.

"Shall we go to the kitchen?" he asked.

"No," Nuts said, kneeling to face Norbert. "First you can prove how much of an expert you really are. If you pass my quiz, you get your sausage roll. If you fail, it's mine."

Norbert narrowed his eyes.

"But I never claimed to know anything," he said.

"Then you shouldn't have swaggered in here shouting your mouth off about how much of a BTC superfan you are. Here's a very simple question. Why has he got a frying pan in that poster?"

Norbert considered diffusing the situation by giving up, and relinquishing the sausage roll. But hunger and a competitive instinct got the better of him. He pondered the potential storylines of a children's book, and reasoned that it was unlikely a talking carrot would cook. After all, other vegetables could be his friends. So he considered what else a frying pan could be used for, and ruled out a violent attack for the target age group.

"Tennis?" he said.

Her nostrils flared and the two of them spent a moment in uneasy silence before she jumped to her feet and stomped past him.

"Dinner time," she said.

"More, more, more..." Nuts said, until the saucepan was empty and her sausage roll was buried under a mountain of baked beans.

"So, how are you two getting on?" Kara asked. "Made any progress?"

"With what? His great big pile of lies?" Nuts asked.

"Thank you for dinner," Norbert added.

"So. Baz tells me you live alone," Kara said. "Where are your parents?"

"They went on holiday, and there was a plane crash."

"Bet there was," Nuts muttered, beans falling from her overloaded fork.

Kara ignored her daughter and continued. "Do you live with your grandparents? Or were you adopted?"

"Yes, my grandmother."

Baz beamed and patted Norbert on the shoulder.

"That's great, Norbert. You must be getting your memory back. Earlier on you said you lived with a robot owl!"

Nuts laughed and a baked bean shot from her nose and splattered on the table. Kara gave her a stern look.

"A robot owl!" she repeated. "Ha ha ha. Baz, where did you find him? In a box marked lunatic?"

"Nuts. You're being rude," Kara said. "Your father used to make robot owls, funnily enough. Norbert had a nasty fall in a building site and lost his memory. He's quite clearly not a lunatic. What's five times ten, Norbert?"

"Fifty," he replied.

"See!" Kara said, with genuine excitement. "We have a genius in our midst."

Norbert narrowed his eyes.

"Call the Hawks and get him back to his robot grandma," Nuts said.

"Why is he our problem?"

"Norbert love, ignore her. You're not a *problem*. Nuts, you're too young to understand."

"No I'm not," she said defiantly. "I'm fifteen. I understand more than all of you lot put together and multiplied by ten. Which I already knew was fifty, by the way."

"Well, there's a 99% chance that the Hawks will reunite Norbert with his parents or grandparents," Kara said.

Norbert set down his knife and fork, a look of concern spreading over his face.

"What's the remaining one percent?" he asked.

"You get disappeared!" Nuts blurted out excitedly.

"NUTS! Go to your room!" Kara shouted.

An awkward silence hung over dessert. Nuts was eventually invited back, but no more was said of disappearances.

"Tomorrow, I'll find out where Westover Street is and we'll get you home. 100%," Kara said.

Norbert nodded, unconvinced by the sudden disappearance of the 1% chance of things going badly.

"Baz, are you working tomorrow, too?" he asked.

Yes, but don't worry. Kara said you can hang out with Nuts, it's school holidays for her. I'll drop you round here in the morning."

As they walked down the hallway, Norbert heard the words 'robot owl', followed a ring of loud laughter. He gulped, and Kara shot him an apologetic look. But unexpectedly, the bedroom door swung open and Nuts held a pile of clothes in outstretched hands.

"Take these," she said. "You look ridiculous."

Norbert gratefully took them from her, and thumbed through a pair of dark grey cargo trousers, what appeared to be a hand-knitted cardigan, and a black T-shirt with a Billy the Carrot logo.

With that, she returned to her lair and slammed the door, and the guys set out back to Tower 28.

Chapter 11

"Nothing to report."

K ara nodded politely to the driver and took her favourite seat at the back of the bus. As the heavy old vehicle grumbled its way through a maze of suburban streets, she watched the buildings get taller and the streets get wider. With a hiss and a clunk, the doors continued to gobble up more passengers and by the time the bus reached the city centre, Kara was well and truly buried, her scarf wrapped around her lower face. The doors swung open for the final time and dozens of passengers spilled into the city centre depot.

She took in a deep breath, making the most of the fresh November air between the bus and the city headquarters, in which she would spend her working day.

Inside the revolving doors was a vast atrium, with staircases and corridors heading off in all directions, like tentacles of an octopus. Kara navigated on auto-pilot down a wide hallway marked HOUSING, and into SOUTHERN DISTRICTS, then up four flights of stairs. Slightly out of breath, she pushed open another set of doors - holding them for her friend Darla who sped up.

"Don't rush for me," joked Kara. "I'm not exactly desperate to start."

Darla looked awkwardly at Kara and nodded. "I am eager to start. I enjoy my job."

Kara raised her eyebrows, and the two went their separate ways. Kara's commute had a certain symmetry to it. First she would bus her way from the tips of the farthest root to the base of the trunk, and then the process would reverse, and she threaded her way down the branch-like corridors until she opened a door marked SOUTHERN DISTRICT DEMOLITION.

"Morning all," she said cheerfully to her six colleagues, who raised their heads from their typewriters and reciprocated the greeting.

"Kettle's just boiled," said Sonita, a dark-haired woman a little younger than Kara. "And, sorry, here are this weeks' files," she added as she passed a stack of pink and yellow papers to Kara.

"Don't apologise, boss. Goes quicker when you're busy, doesn't it."

Kara slid a framed photo of Nuts to the side to make room for the thick slab of paperwork, which she placed next to her typewriter.

The morning was spent quietly working her way through demolition reports, which had to be carefully stamped and filed under the street name. At 10am Imogen - the youngest team member, who was always eager to please - filled the kettle. She set out six mugs, placed tea bags in four of them and spooned coffee into the other two.

Kara joined her by the kettle and said quietly, "Not for me today."

"Really? I've never known you turn down a cup of tea."

"Well, I've got to pop out. I need to see a friend of mine," Kara said mysteriously. Sid, a particularly nosey colleague, cocked his head to one side and watched her slip out through the office door.

Kara worked her way out of the housing department and through a heavy set of doors marked POLICE. She kept her eyes down and avoided making contact with Hawks, in their dark blue uniforms. Kara entered through a set of doors with MISSING PERSONS in large black letters. A serious-looking woman at reception asked her to sign in, but Kara said she was not here on official business and had just come to give something to her friend. The receptionist nodded reluctantly, and Kara continued her journey through a maze of desks until she reached a familiar face tucked away in a far corner.

"Kara, how are you?" The woman asked, clearly surprised to have a visitor. "Is everything okay?"

The room bustled with people ferrying paperwork and taking phone calls. Kara crouched down by her friend's desk and began.

"Hello Hilts. Sorry to bother you. I have a question."

She stood to peer over the top of the wooden screen around Hilta's cubicle, and seeing nobody was walking by, Kara continued.

"Have you heard about a kid going missing recently? About 12 or 13."

"I don't think so," said Hilta. "I always notice when a kid goes missing, but let me look."

Hilta stood and brought down a cardboard box from a shelf, and flicked through the sheets of paper which filled it.

"This goes back two weeks, and I don't see any children at all. What's the case number?"

Kara checked again for anyone nearby, and leaned in close to her friend.

"There is no case number. Not yet. It's…it's an odd one."

Hilta sat at her desk and glanced around her office nervously. Her voice was now a whisper.

"What do you mean, no case number? Has this child been reported missing or not? Who are the parents?"

Kara's face went red with nerves, and she stood and smiled.

"Nothing, Hilta. It's probably nothing. Just Nuts said something about a girl he'd heard about, through the grapevine. And I was curious, and passing by and I thought I'd stop in and say hello. Perhaps you and the girls can come round for dinner next week?" Her voice returned to its regular volume with the last sentence, as though to reassure anyone listening that they were having a perfectly normal conversation.

"Yes, that would be nice. I really must get on." Hilta stood up to return the box file. If you come back please give the case number to the receptionist, rather than coming back to see me. There are procedures for a reason!"

Kara apologised and swiftly saw herself out, returning to her office, where she noticed Sid peek round the corner of his cubicle as she returned to her desk.

"Ah Kara, you're back. Do you know if the property on Manor Road got demolished?" Sonita asked.

"What is the big fuss about Manor Road?" asked Sid. He dipped his glasses and peered around his stack of demolition reports. "In my fourteen years in this room I don't think I've ever had so much interest in a property from up high."

Sonita ignored him.

"Can you find out, Kara, please? It was Barry. Sid, I can literally see your ears twitching!" Sonita snapped.

Sid stood up. "Sorry, but nothing happens in this room. So when we get a flurry of red papers then yes my ears are going to twitch. What is so important that this house needs demolishing on a Saturday, of all things. Then it's so critical that they follow up at 9:04am on Monday morning to check it happened."

"Please, Sid!" Sonita said firmly. "If there's one thing we know, it's not to ask questions. Do I need to report you for asking questions?"

"No, Sonita." Sid's head bowed down to the floor and he slunk back behind his desk, pressing his fingertips softly on the keys of his typewriter so as to not make any noise.

"I actually had dinner with Baz last night, and yes it got demolished fine."

"Good. Nothing to report? No issues at all?" Sonita asked.

"None."

Chapter 12

"Is this a test?"

Afer much knocking, Nuts opened the front door of her flat, then immediately closed it in Norbert's face. A second later she reopened it and he followed her through to the kitchen. She poured cereal into her mouth, straight from the box, giving a thumbs up to his (her) outfit.

"Thanks for these," he said, pinching the fabric on a pair of black combat trousers.

"If you annoy me, I'm taking them back," Nuts said.

"Could be awkward," he muttered. Norbert took an egg from his pockets and placed it on the kitchen table. "This is for you."

"An egg!" Nuts said, holding it up reverently like it was made of solid gold. "Where did you get it?"

"Baz told me to bring it, and not to mention it to anyone but you."

Nuts eyed him suspiciously, and he felt on edge.

"What?" he asked, palms up.

"Where did you *really* get the egg?" she said, arms folded. "You're in Trixie's Little Helpers, aren't you."

Before he knew what was happening, she pounced on him and pinned him against the linoleum floor. Norbert shrieked, frozen in a state of shock as she rifled through his pockets, which were empty.

"Get off! I don't even know who Trixie is," he said, rolling onto his side to shove her off.

"Said no-one, ever," she replied, drawing back.

They returned to their places at the table, both still cautious of the other. Nuts rolled the egg across the table to him, which he was rather pleased to catch.

"Eat it!" she demanded.

"Is this a test?" he asked, inspecting the egg.

"You're a spy. It's plain as day. You showed up out of nowhere and you're here to trick me into eating contraband. You want to put me in jail."

The ticking of an old fashioned wall clock cranked up the tension in the room. Nuts stared at Norbert with a self-satisfied smile, her chin resting on a cradle of interlocked fingers. For Norbert, the whole scene felt ridiculous.

"Nuts, if I was so deep undercover that I was willing to hide in a building being smashed to the ground, would I really worry about eating an egg?"

"Prove it!" she said.

Norbert picked the shell from the egg and gobbled it up in two cheek-swelling bites.

Nuts sank back into her chair. "I wanted that," she said.

"Nuts, I've got to get home. Can you help me?" Norbert asked.

"So you can meet your robot owl?" she sniggered.

"Yes. He's not a robot. He's my friend. And I have to search for my parents. We're at the cusp of a breakthrough. Have you heard of Blackstone High?"

She shook her head.

"Have you heard of Carston City?" he asked.

She shook her head.

"Do you have the internet?"

"What is that?" she asked.

"All the computers in the world, talking to each other," he explained. "A vast network."

She looked blank.

"We have normal stuff," she said, slightly exasperated. "Carpet. Windows. Plants. We don't have robots and computers."

"We, as in, you and your mum? Or we, as in, everyone?"

"I've never heard of a computer," she said.

Norbert narrowed his eyes, wondering if she was messing with him. He knew only of a world where computers were in everything, from phones to televisions. Even his kettle was connected to the internet, and could be told to boil water without him getting out of bed. With that in mind, he began to search Nuts' flat for evidence of modern technology while she watched him curiously.

The television was a hulking grey cube and looked like if it fell off its stand, it would punch a hole through the floor. Nuts had no games console or laptop. Even the clock on the oven had old-fashioned hands that rotated around a dial.

"See, I told you," Nuts said. "It's boring here."

"Baz told me to stay put," Norbert said nervously. "Can we phone your mum and ask if she's found anything out? Maybe she's located my house."

Nuts held the phone away from her mouth so they could both hear the conversation. After being passed between several receptionists, she heard the warm voice of her mum.

"Are you hurt?" Kara said, panic in her voice. "What happened? Your arm? Legs!?"

"I'm fine, mum. Did you find anything out?"

"Oh. I can't speak, I'm at work. I'll talk to you later," she said, the discomfort clear in her voice.

"Anything?"

"Your lunch is in the fridge," Kara said.

Nuts put her hand over the mouthpiece. "She's doing her fake voice, like she's a game show host."

"Ask her questions she can answer with yes or no," Norbert whispered.

Nuts cleared her throat.

"Is Norbert on the missing persons list?" she asked quietly.

"No. Your pie is on the top shelf, darling. Next to the mustard," Kara said, with a hint of laughter.

"Did you find out where Westover Street is?" Nuts asked.

"No. That's right, honey. Just put the oven on full whack and give it ten minutes."

"You what? I'm asking about Westover Street. It doesn't exist?" Nuts said. "Or you didn't find a map yet?"

"No. If it's not on the shelf, then it's not there. *It doesn't exist.* Look, I have to go now. See you at six."

Nuts put the phone down, then picked it up again to check it had definitely disconnected.

"She wasn't making sense, but I think you don't exist," she said. "Nor does Westover Street. Sorry."

Norbert sat heavily on a dining chair and stared into space, trying to process the information. He wasn't surprised that he hadn't been reported missing. After all, Owly knew he liked to keep a low profile, and wouldn't have phoned the police. Not yet, not after only a few days. But the fact that Westover Road wasn't on any map didn't make any sense, and nor did the total lack of internet.

Nuts opened the fridge and rooted around on the top shelf.

"There's no pie," she said. "I don't get it."

Norbert shook his head.

Nuts wheeled her bicycle along the gangway outside the flat. Beneath them, a pigeon circled the canyon that formed between the tower blocks.

"Baz said to keep inside and lie low. Is going out a good idea?" Norbert asked.

"No," Nuts said, the straps of a crash helmet swinging by her cheeks. "But good ideas are overrated."

She continued past the lifts and kicked open the door to the stairwell. Norbert looked over the bannister at a gloomy spiral that descended fourteen storeys to the ground. Nuts sat on her bike and clipped her crash helmet shut.

"Are you crazy?" he asked.

She nodded, kicked at the pedals and began rumbling down the stairs. At each platform, she skidded the bike violently toward the next set, gathering speed until she was a blur. Norbert watched with a mixture of terror and intense envy as she zig-zagged down the jagged concrete mountain. He jogged down to find her barely out of breath, casually holding the door open for him.

"How was that?" Norbert asked excitedly.

Nuts shrugged, and pushed her bike alongside Norbert so the two of them could talk, crash helmet swinging from the handlebars.

"Where are we going?" he asked.

"When cats get lost, they walk in a big spiral until they find something they recognise. Let's do that," she said.

It seemed like a sensible enough plan, so they began ambling around the streets. Norbert searched desperately for something familiar, but found only concrete. Dank grey underpasses that flickered with green light. Tower blocks so monstrous that they blocked the sun, linked with a spider web of pedestrian bridges.

And yet through the endless urban sprawl, nature fought back. Trees erupted through pavements like slow motion volcanoes. Now and then, Nuts mounted her bicycle and used the angular slabs of concrete as launch ramps.

"Do you recognise anything?" Nuts asked.

Norbert shook his head, sadly.

"Do you remember if you could see the wall from your house?" she asked.

"What wall?"

She sniggered, then her face straightened when she realised Norbert was genuinely clueless.

"Come with me, egg spy," she said, swinging her leg over the saddle and motioning for Norbert to hop onto the footpegs. "If we don't leave now, we'll never make it before mum gets home."

Not for the first time, Norbert was unsure of their destination, but dutifully climbed aboard Nuts' BMX.

"Be careful, alright?" he said. "I'm not getting on well with bikes at the moment."

Chapter 13

"What's beyond the wall?"

"Can you slow down a little? You're going too fast," he pleaded, as Nuts jumped from the pavement to the road.

"Zip it, Norbert!" she shouted back as they came over the brow of a hill. "We're going too fast for chit-chat."

Norbert clung on with every ounce of his strength as they picked up speed. Nuts shifted back in her saddle and raised the front wheel off the ground, her knees swinging this way and that to keep balanced. Norbert clamped his eyes tight shut and squeezed her so tight he became her backpack.

"It wheelies so *sweet* with you on the back!" she shouted, ecstatic at her stunt.

Norbert felt the road surface change from stone to gravel and the undulations of a path made his stomach lurch. He bravely opened one of his eyes and saw that the tower blocks had gone, and they were on a path that rollercoastered through a forest. His legs ached from standing on the footpegs, and he was grateful when he saw a flash of white between the trees. At first, he thought it was the sky, but it seemed, impossibly, to be even bigger.

The bike burst into a clearing and skidded to a stop, spraying gravel up at a sheer concrete cliff face. Nuts vaulted off and Norbert, still frozen in fear, simply fell to the ground like a tree in a storm.

"Did you enjoy the ride?" she asked.

Norbert lay face up, wiping his mouth on his sleeve to remove some dirt. As his eyes opened, he stared directly up at the wall, which seemed to go up and up forever. He sat up, looking one way and then the other, to find that the wall faded out of sight in every direction.

"Wow," he said. "That's the biggest wall I've ever seen. What is it for?"

"It's the edge, the boundary of Puzzle Forest. Seriously, you've forgotten the wall?" Nuts laughed. "I've hit my head approximately once a day for fifteen years and even I remember the wall."

Norbert climbed to his feet and ran his fingers along the rough white concrete.

"Tell me more about Puzzle Forest and why there's a huge wall around it."

Norbert sat with his back to the wall while Nuts scurried this way and that, gathering sticks and handfuls of dirt. To his left and right, the wall appeared to be razor-straight, but when the clouds cleared he could faintly make out the top, and its gentle inward curve. In front of the wall was a strip of dirt that separated it from the dark forest they had cycled through. He felt as if he were in a dream. The skyscrapers, the radiation, the wall; none of them fit into his world view, and the scale of these things was overwhelming.

"There," Nuts said, proudly. She slapped her hands together to wipe them clean.

A cluster of sticks were jammed into the ground, surrounded by a bed of moss in a loose circle. The circumference of the whole city was marked out in fragments of bark.

She waved a stick in a wide circle, to indicate the extent of her known universe.

"This is Puzzle Forest," she began. "The sticks in the middle are the buildings in the city centre. There are big tall buildings where my mum works, right in the centre. Shops and stuff. Then there are houses, fancy ones first, then the tower blocks like where I live."

Norbert nodded.

"The city is surrounded by forest, miles and miles deep. That's the moss. And at the edge of the forest is the wall, which is the bark. You have to imagine it's really high."

Norbert raised a hand, like he was in school. Nuts laughed.

"What's beyond the wall? Where is Puzzle Forest," he asked.

'She sat down and scratched her head.

"How much time do we have?" she joked, glancing at her watch for effect.

Her face fell, and she examined it again.

"Aagh, we have to go. My mum will be on the bus back from the city. We have to get home before she does. We were meant to stay indoors."

Nuts picked up her bike and swung the pedal round, ready to begin. Norbert scrambled onto the foot pegs and held on. He watched the wall disappear out of sight as they re-entered the dense forest.

"Nuts, what's beyond the wall?" he shouted.

She shook her head, stamping forcefully on the pedals, the bike fishtailing along the gravel path.

"Not now, Norbert. I told you we should have stayed home!"

"Norbert *made* me!" Nuts said, her hands upturned to demonstrate she had nothing to hide. "I wanted to stay home."

Kara gave a fake laugh and continued washing up, dumping plates and cups into the sink so angrily that water splashed onto her skirt. Norbert stood meekly in the corner of the kitchen, staring at the floor. He had lived alone for over a year, and even in the first ten years of his life, his parents had never been shouters. He recalled a time when his mum was 'disappointed' when he had dismantled the toaster in search of a component he needed. That was about as heated as it had got in Norbert's household. Or not heated, in the case of the broken toaster.

"Anyway, Norbert, we have to talk," Kara said seriously, scraping a chair back and kicking off her work shoes.

"You haven't been reported as missing. The street name you told us doesn't exist. Nor does Blackstone High. It's time for you to tell me the truth."

Norbert shrugged helplessly.

"I don't know what to tell you. I'm not lying. It's possible I lost my memory but I don't think so."

"He's not lying," Nuts confirmed, with arms-crossed authority. "I gave him a test this morning. He passed."

Kara sighed impatiently.

"Think carefully. Who do you live with?" she asked.

"Owly," he said.

"The robot. Of course. But who else? Your grandparents? Your carers?"

"Nobody. My parents went on holiday and their plane crashed into the Asantic Ocean, but they survived," he said.

"When?"

"A year ago."

"That's impossible," she said.

"It's not. I built a replica plane and crashed it into the lake. It proved they could have survived."

"What's the last thing you remember before Baz woke you up?" she asked.

"I was in the toilets at my school, hiding from Dani. She's the worst person in the world. She was beating me up, so I climbed out of the window. I stole her bike,"

"Why did you steal her bike?" Nuts asked.

"I don't know. I just did. It was snowing. I didn't want to go home because I thought she'd hunt me down at my house, so I went into the woods to hide. But I got lost and I think I crashed. That's the last thing I remember before I woke up, all wet in the basement."

Kara put her head in her hands.

"I don't know what to do, Norbert. If I call the Hawks, they'll ask you all the same questions as me, and I don't think they'll like your answers. I want to believe you, hon. But this talk of planes and owls; it's just madness."

"Will I get...disappeared?" he asked. His lip quivered slightly.

"Yup!" Nuts said.

Kara whacked her daughter with a straw place mat.

"Honestly, I don't know what would happen, Norbert, but I'm not about to find out. Stay with me or Baz, and we'll keep figuring it out, okay?"

He nodded.

"What's beyond the wall?" he asked.

Nuts and Kara looked at each other.

"Nothing," Kara said. "Wasteland."

"What do you mean?"

"Nuts, I have to make dinner. It's time Norbert knew the truth about the outside world. Take him to your room and explain."

Chapter 14

"Seventeen what?"

Nuts pulled a picture book from her shelf and tapped the carpet to invite Norbert to join her. He was quite touched, since only yesterday she had shouted at him for moving a toy.

"I know it's a Billy the Carrot book, but that's how I get all my information," she said.

Norbert already looked concerned. The first page showed a smartly dressed business woman, looking out of her office over a huge city encircled by forest. Ridiculous shoulder pads, leopard print trouser suit. Norbert recognised her as the blonde woman from the calendar.

"That's Trixie, the world's youngest billionaire. She's our saviour."

"Why is she in a Billy the Carrot book?" Norbert asked.

"She's in all books," Nuts said.

The next page showed an advert for Puzzle Forest, in which a happy couple pushed a pram down an immaculate tree-lined street.

"She built Puzzle Forest, which, as you know, has the city centre with all the skyscrapers, then all the houses and tower blocks, and finally the forest. It was built before you and I were born. But my mum remembers moving in. She was brought up outside."

"What year was it built?" Norbert asked. "Surely I would remember it."

"It was zero, obviously. Trixie restarted the clock."

"What?" Norbert asked, staring at Nuts in disbelief.

"Shush. Just listen to the story," Nuts said. "Trixie built the biggest wall in the world to keep everyone inside safe," Nuts said.

"From what?" Norbert asked.

"Concrete."

"No, I mean, what is she keeping us safe from?"

Nuts' eyes lit up. "That's her genius! She saw it coming."

The next page made Norbert shriek. A blood red illustration showed a world in ruin. A desolate road was littered with abandoned cars, skeletons slumped over their steering wheels. Buildings were burned down to rubble and trees stood limp and lifeless.

"The great apocalypse," Nuts said dramatically. "Do you know about that?"

Norbert shook his head.

"Twenty years ago, almost," Nuts continued. "A radiation leak at a power plant wiped everything. Animals, humans, even insects. Nothing survived except the people inside Puzzle Forest, who were protected by the wall."

"How did a wall protect people from radiation?" Norbert asked.

Nuts stared at him. "It's thick. And it worked, because we're all alive."

He took the book from Nuts and studied the scenes of destruction. He thought of the pigeon he had seen swooping under the tower block, and wondered about the fates of elephants and kangaroos.

"Does your mum remember it happening?" Norbert asked.

"I do," Kara said.

The kids hadn't realised Kara was watching them from the doorway with red eyes.

"I'm sorry," Norbert said.

"It's okay, hon," she said. "But as Nuts explained; unless you built a time-machine, which I think you'd remember, you were born in Puzzle Forest. You must have got a knock on the head and got your address and school name wrong, which can happen. Nuts has said some ridiculous things after a fall, haven't you, love?"

"Nope," she said. "There was, like, one time I went over the handlebars and thought I liked apples. But I've never once claimed to live with a magic owl."

"Okay, okay," Kara said. "Come in for your dinner."

"Kara, what year is it?" Norbert asked.

"Seventeen," she said.

"Seventeen what? It's January 2032, right?" Norbert asked.

Kara stopped what she was doing and glared at Norbert, shaking her head.

"Seventeen years since Trixie saved us all," Nuts chimed in.

"Not mad 'Trixie' years. What is the *real* year?" Norbert continued, a little agitated.

Nuts slapped a palm over Norbert's mouth, silencing him. The phone rang.

With a shaking hand, Kara picked up. Norbert could not hear what was being said, but just watched Kara nod, and say yes, several times.

"I'm sorry, it was just my daughter playing a silly game," she said. "I'll be sure to tell her not to joke around like that."

She placed the phone back on its hook and returned to her task of dolloping mashed potato onto plates. An eerie silence fell across the kitchen.

Norbert mouthed the words 'What is going on?', to which Nuts simply placed a finger on her lips. On a chalkboard on the wall, Norbert scribbled 'Are they listening?'

Nuts took the stick of chalk from him and wrote 'Certain words. Don't talk about the old world', then wiped it all off with a rag.

Everyone took their seats at the table and picked up their cutlery, acting as if the call had never happened.

"Yay, I love mash," Nuts said, scraping it into a volcano shape in preparation for the gravy.

Norbert, shaken at the thought of people listening to their conversations, quietly copied her. He created a twisting helter-skelter of potato, which Kara said looked impressive and Nuts knocked down, jealously.

There was no more talk of the year.

Back at Baz's flat, Norbert lay awake, staring at the ceiling. He could hear Baz snoring through the wall, but that wasn't what kept him awake.

He felt for a lamp shade in the dark, locating a little round knob with his fingertips. He cupped it with his other hand to muffle the click as it came on. The clock on the wall read quarter past two. He carefully folded the purple blanket and placed it on the side table. In the kitchen he quietly opened a drawer and found a pencil. "Thanks for everything" he wrote on a slip of kitchen roll.

He released the door latch ever so gently and stepped into the snowy night. As he walked along the gangway, the tower blocks looked more menacing than ever. Norbert took the stairs, not wanting to wake any of the residents with the whirr of the lift.

At the foot of the building, he trudged through a snowy park toward a wall of trees, carefully retracing the route he had taken with Nuts that afternoon. A challenge, since he had spent a lot of that journey with his eyes tight shut.

The walk through the forest took nearly two hours, and he blew on his hands to keep them warm. At times he lost the trail, but managed to find it again by searching for tyre tracks left by Nuts earlier on. Any later and they too, would have become buried by fresh snow.

The wall was no less spectacular the second time around. A vast cliff of concrete, lit white by the moon and soaring so high that it made the oak trees near the base look like matchsticks. Norbert heard a rustling and darted into the cover of a bush. He peered back at the forest but saw nothing but branches which had long since lost their leaves for winter.

Looking along the wall he found the small fence he had spotted earlier, and he set toward it. Protected in a cage was a white ladder bolted to the wall, which reached into the milky night sky until it became invisible.

Norbert placed his fingers through the chain link fence, unsure for a moment whether the metal was freezing his fingers or zapping them with electric current. A black and yellow sign rattled.

'Warning. Danger of Death and Imprisonment. Trixico Employees ONLY.'

He climbed to the top of the head-height fence and reached across for the ladder, grabbing an icy rung. He stretched the sleeves of his jumper over his hands to stop them sticking to the metal, but now his concern became whether they could provide sufficient grip. With every step, the view down to the ground got more dizzying, and once he was above the height of the trees, he forbade himself from looking.

Step by step, he moved up the ladder, his limbs frozen and shaking. He imagined the Hawks finding his body, curled up at the foot of the ladder, with no identification. If a boy falls in a forest and nobody hears, does he really exist?

At about twice the height of the trees, he heard a bang near his head. Norbert froze, wondering for a moment if he had imagined it, before another rock clattered near his head. A figure peered up at him from the ground and panic set in.

It must be a Hawk, he thought, and therefore he must run. As he reached for the next rung, a voice made it through the night air saying his name. He chewed over the sound, low and gruff. It was Baz.

Norbert climbed down the ladder, returning to the enclosure inside the fence at the bottom.

"What are you doing Norbert?" whispered Baz. He wore pyjamas, boots and a hat. "They'll take you away if they catch you out on the wall. Get back. Please Norbert, for me. You have to trust me on this. You do not want to get taken by the Hawks."

Baz rattled the fence, his face distraught.

"I can't go back with you, Baz," Norbert replied. "This isn't my home. Kara has checked, and my life isn't inside this wall. If it's not inside, it must be outside. I'm from Carston City, and it must be this way."

He pointed up.

"No, no, no, Norbert. There is nothing outside that wall except death. Carston City is gone. You'll die out there."

"Baz, I was there a couple of days ago and can assure you I'll be fine."

"Says the boy who I found in a basement, in a coffin," Baz said. "Come with me. Now! You can stay at my house and I won't take you to the city. You can just hang out there until we figure out a plan. Don't climb the ladder. Nobody ever, ever comes back from it. I'll tell you more when we get home. We shouldn't be talking here."

Norbert looked up at the ladder, then back at Baz.

They walked home in silence, picking a path through the forest to keep off the roads. By the time they reached the tower blocks, both of them were shaking with cold, too tired to even brush the snow from their hair.

"Thanks for coming to get me. You didn't have to," said Norbert as he pulled the purple blanket up to his chin. Baz nodded and turned out the light, falling asleep on the armchair in the lounge.

Chapter 15

"We're the lucky ones."

Norbert woke up to the sound of a mug chinking onto a ceramic coaster. Baz slid the curtain back on its pole and light flooded the lounge.

"I need to tell you more about Puzzle Forest," he said. "I don't want to see you getting put in jail before you've had a chance to start looking for your home."

Norbert picked up his hot cup of tea and shrouded it in his fingertips. The coaster featured a photograph of Trixie, wearing purple eye-shadow with matching lipstick. In curly handwritten font it said 'Our Saviour'.

"The walls are there to keep us safe. That's the deal with Puzzle Forest. We're the lucky ones. The last survivors. Beyond that wall is nothing but sickness and death."

Norbert chewed the inside of his lip as he tried to make sense of this.

"That's what Nuts said, but it was in a picture book and I didn't really believe her. So you're saying the whole world is decimated?" he said. "Since when?"

Baz nodded solemnly.

"Seventeen years. Trixie has made sure the walls are high enough that we're all safe in here. Beyond the walls there is nothing. I've seen video on the television of the world outside. It's a desert. A wasteland. Just red rocks and skulls. No birds in the sky. Not even an ant on the ground. That's why I came to get you. I don't know what I was more scared of; the Hawks slinging you in jail, or you getting to the top of the wall and getting disintegrated."

Norbert thought for a few minutes before asking "What will they do with a lone kid, in this place? Where will they put me?"

"I don't know," Baz answered honestly. "But Kara asked around in the city, and there's no report of a boy going missing."

"I told you. My parents are missing too. So should I go and hand myself in?" he said.

Baz shook his head and put a hand onto Norbert's wrist.

"Don't do that. Not yet. When I found you, I assumed your parents would be worried sick and wanted to reunite you. But if what you say is right, then I don't want to risk putting you in the care of the..."

Baz did the motion of wings, flapping. He continued speaking quietly.

"Me and Kara think it's best to do some more digging first. The house I demolished on the weekend is unusual, because it's old and different to the others. We have to find out whose house it was, and maybe that'll give us some clues as to why you were there. Maybe your home is near that one."

Norbert nodded, but didn't really understand how that would help. Sometimes Baz and Kara talked about the Hawks as their saviours and protectors, and sometimes they seemed terrified to say their name out loud.

"The thing is, Norbert. I'm sure the Hawks would take you away and find a nice home for you, which is good. They could find your parents, or a lovely new family. So there's nothing to worry about."

"But?" Norbert said.

Baz grabbed Norbert's leaving note from the table and scribbled on the reverse side. With barely a flash, he showed it to Norbert. It read 'Don't trust Hawks'. He then screwed the whole thing into a tight ball and threw it into the bin.

"In the meantime you can stay with me," Baz said. "Help yourself to whatever you can find in the fridge. The telly's broken but there are some books. If you do go out, for your sake and mine, keep a low profile. Avoid hanging out with Nuts. We can't have you getting busted."

Baz looked seriously at Norbert and waited for the little guy to nod in agreement. Satisfied, he smiled and gave Norbert's mousy brown hair a fatherly ruffle.

"Sorry for getting you up in the night," Norbert said.

"No problem kiddo. I got my daily run in before my alarm went off. I'm training for Shadow Runners."

Norbert looked at him blankly.

"I'll tell you about that later," Baz said.

Two hours of staring at tower blocks and pondering his own existence was enough for Norbert, so he decided to fix the television. He was grateful for Baz's hospitality, and felt guilty about dragging the poor guy on a rescue mission in his pyjamas. Fixing the TV was the least he could do.

He unplugged the heavy black box and rotated it so the screen faced the wall. Norbert counted eight pencil-sized holes, and deep within them he could make out the glint of criss-crossed screw heads. Baz had a collection of tools in the hallway and Norbert quickly found a screwdriver and got to work. Holding both sides of the appliance, he pulled off the back to reveal a dusty jungle of wires and circuit boards.

Norbert peered into the device, drinking in every detail of the green plastic boards, etched with geometric copper rivers. Capacitors and resistors clung like insects on grass, their wire legs ending in shiny silver boots. Electrons poured from one plateau to another in a waterfall of neat, colourful wires. For Norbert, it was as beautiful as any television program he might see on the screen. It reminded him of home, and he rubbed his hands together in excitement.

He traced the incoming black cable which led from the plug at the wall, and followed the wire as it split again and again, feeding into different parts of the circuit. He got a pencil and started to jot down what each part was doing, until he had drawn what looked like a railway map, covering several sheets of kitchen roll.

There was a knock at the door.

"This is insane," Nuts said, rotating the kitchen roll diagram. Norbert politely returned it to the table, where it completed a jigsaw that only he understood.

"Nuts, you have the same television, right?" Norbert said.

"Of course. Everyone does," she said. "Why? Don't tell me. I bet you have a magic one that flies or something."

He shook his head.

"No, but this style of television is really old. No offence. These days televisions are so thin you can hang them on the wall like pictures. Light emitting diodes. This is a cathode..."

Nuts plugged her ears with the tips of her fingers and shook her head.

"Please, Norbert. Stop! It's the school holidays. You sound like a teacher."

Deep inside the television, Norbert spotted a dead moth, its body frazzled into a charred lump.

"That's the issue," he said, placing it onto the table. "It caused a short."

"What's a short?" Nuts asked. "Actually I don't care."

Before reassembling the television, he noticed a little dial inside about the size of a wristwatch. Curiously, it had a plastic cable tie which locked it in place, preventing it from rotating. It was strange, Norbert thought, that anybody would design a television with a rotating component and then jam something in place so that it cannot rotate. He assumed it had been added after the television was manufactured and rebelliously snipped through it with a pair of pliers.

He plugged the television back in and to his delight, the screen burst into life.

"Finally," Nuts said. "Can we go out now?

"Sorry Nuts, but is it okay if I take a shower first?"

She screamed and stormed out of the door.

"I'll be doing laps of the stairs," she yelled behind her.

Chapter 16

"A cockroach crawls out from under a rock."

N orbert and Nuts crossed the footbridge which linked their tower blocks. A chain link fence wrapped up and over them, like a tunnel, and the shadowy pattern of hexagons carpeted the concrete floor.

"Reminds me of a hamster cage I had once," Norbert said.

"What's a hamster?" Nuts asked.

"Like a mouse, but bigger. People have them as pets."

"A rat?" she said, with genuine excitement.

"Cuter than a rat. Fluffier, rounder. But yes, same family."

"I have a pet rat," Nuts said. This came as a surprise to Norbert, who had visited her bedroom several times.

Beneath them, a bin lorry crawled down the street, beeping constantly as its workers slung black sacks into its hungry jaws. Nuts pointed down toward a cluster of filthy dumpsters, which were fed by chutes from her tower block.

"She lives in there," Nuts said. "She's called Vermina."

Suddenly she stopped, and her face fell. At the far end of the walkway was a girl of about the same age.

"Oh drat," Nuts said. "Anna." She looked urgently at Norbert and whispered "Don't say a word! Nothing. I'll do the talking."

They walked in silence to the end of the footbridge where Anna blocked their path. She wore a navy blazer, criss-crossed by scarlet stripes. Her black hair wrapped around her neck in an immaculate bob, and in her hands she held a clipboard and pen.

"Hello Nutella. Who is this?" the girl asked.

"None of your business. Why are you wearing school uniform in the holidays?"

"Because it's comfortable. It's smart. I'm doing an important study for the architecture department. Not all of us want to dress like we crawled through a jumble sale and hoped for the best," Anna said, looking Norbert up and down.

"Well?" she said. "Who are you?"

Norbert kept quiet and looked to Nuts to rescue him.

"He's a friend," Nuts said. "You wouldn't understand."

"I don't know him," Anna said.

"He's not in our year," Nuts said.

"He's not in our school. I memorised everyone's photos for my Head Girl application. Can he talk for himself?"

Nuts pushed past Anna, dragging Norbert with him by the wrist.

"Go and do a sudoku, Anna," Nuts shouted back.

When the lift doors closed, Nuts shook her head.

"That's Anna," she said.

"I got that," Norbert replied. "Should we be worried?"

"No. She's just..." Nuts searched for the words to describe Anna. The lift doors reopened and Norbert followed along the gangway to the front door, where Nuts jabbed her key at the hole over and over again, chipping blue paint as she missed. Eventually Norbert gently inserted it into the lock and let them in. Nuts flopped onto the sofa in the way Norbert had become accustomed to. She didn't put her hands out to brace her fall or even close her eyes. Just collapsed like a felled tree. Norbert sat on the floor.

"Norbert, imagine the end of the world," Nuts said.

"I mean, that's where we're at, isn't it?"

"No, proper end of the world. Outside the walls. Life stamped out by a gigantic boot that squirms and crushes the life out of everything with a heartbeat. But then a cockroach crawls out from under a rock. That's Anna."

Norbert nodded. The flat was silent but for Nuts' laboured breathing.

"Do you have sudoku? I do actually like puzzles," he said, trying to break the tension.

Nuts hurled a cushion at him and laughed.

"And my mum says I can't look after myself!" Nuts said, grinning as she set a plate on the dining table.

On it was a single slice of bread under a pile of cold baked beans. When Nuts turned to fetch her own lunch, Norbert picked out fragments of plastic wrapper from the pile of grated cheese.

"Your mum would be very proud," he said.

The phone rang, and Kara spoke so loudly that Norbert heard the whole conversation.

"I'm just checking you two are safe at home, and haven't gone out causing mischief," she said.

"No, we're just having beans on untoasted toast. Which I made myself," Nuts said.

"That's fantastic!" Kara said. "You opened a tin? I hope you didn't cut yourself."

Nuts slipped her bandaged finger into her pocket. She wrapped up the call and scooped up the empty plates, setting them by the sink.

"I'll wash up," Norbert said.

"No need," Nuts said. "If you leave it by the sink, it ends up back in the cupboards. I don't really know how it works."

"Magic?" Norbert said, turning on the tap and squirting washing up liquid into a plastic bowl.

Nuts shrugged. "So, how do you know what to do with the television? Are you, like, a genius?"

"My mum is an architect. My dad is a physics teacher. We were always making things in our house."

"I'm a genius, too," Nuts said.

Norbert nodded politely.

"How do you know?" he said, rinsing the bean juice from the plates and stacking them neatly on the draining board rack.

"At school I get my very own teacher, most of the time, and they take me to a special room and I get to do whatever I want. Colouring. Word searches. I think they're worried that I might say something so smart that the other kids' brains explode. Also there was this one time when I got distracted by a butterfly and jumped out of the window."

"I did that, once," Norbert said.

"Brains exploding or window?"

Norbert made the motion of swinging open a window, then did a little hop forward.

"That's when this all went wrong," he sighed, before recounting the story of the toilet episode. As the words came out, Nuts balled her fists in anger and shook her head. Norbert felt a sense of relief to feel heard. The only other person he had spoken to about Blackstone High was Owly, who tended to offer murderous but impractical solutions.

"Norbert, you promise to keep this secret?" Nuts shouted through her bedroom door.

After the required assurances were called back from the hallway, Nuts leapt out of her room.

"Ta da!" she exclaimed proudly.

Nuts spread her arms out wide to reveal an outfit that looked like a Halloween bat costume. A quarter-circle of plastic sheeting connected her arms to her torso, like wings. Another triangle of material connected the inside her legs. She did a few star jumps to demonstrate the opening of her wings, which made a loud rustling noise.

"It's really cool, Nuts. What's it for?"

"BASE jumping! I'm going to be a flying squirrel."

Norbert's eyes opened in alarm.

"What's BASE jumping?" he asked.

"It's like skydiving, except you jump off a building, antenna, span, earth. B, A, S, E. Span means bridge, but they didn't want to call it BABE diving because it doesn't sound as cool."

"So you have a parachute?" Norbert asked.

"No, but my plan is to use the wings to glide down to a safe stop."

Norbert put his head in his hands, peeking through a gap between his fingers.

"How do you know it will work? Have you calculated if that's enough surface area to give you sufficient air resistance?"

"Yes, of course," Nuts said. "I'm not stupid."

She returned to her room and closed the door. After some rustling noises and what Norbert assumed was a box being slid under a bed, Nuts re-emerged in her normal clothes; jeans and a hoodie.

"What's air resistance?" she said.

"Well, if you have too little plastic sheeting for the mass of your body, then you'll just fall like a stone."

Nuts went into the lounge and turned on the television, on which a woman with frizzy blond hair and unusually large eyes sat at a desk. Trixie, Norbert said to himself.

"You are the lucky few, who survived the end of the world," she said.

"This is the good bit," Nuts said, turning up the volume.

The screen changed to a blood red montage of the world beyond the city walls. Rotting fish afloat on the surface of an oily lake. A hundred blackbirds scattered on a road like peppercorns. Norbert stared at the television with a growing sense of horror. He had seen the illustrations in Nuts' book, but he hadn't believed any of it until he saw the footage. It made him feel sick.

"Why are the lakes covered in oil?" Norbert asked.

"Radiation," Nuts said. She turned off the television. "So anyway, is this suit going to work or not. Give me the honest truth," she said.

"No."

"No you won't tell me, or no you don't know?" she said.

"It won't work. There's no way that will slow you down enough to survive," he said. "Think about how big a parachute is. You need that much surface area, not just little wings."

"Yeah but my arms are only so long," she said.

"Right, and maybe that's why humans use planes instead of building wing costumes to get from A to B."

Nuts sighed. "Planes are long gone. Anyway, wings work for birds, don't they? You don't have a growth mindset, Norbert. You're being a negative noo."

"A growth mindset won't change physics. I'm sorry Nuts, I just don't want to see you die."

She smiled. "Aww. Is it because I made you lunch?"

"Nuts, you're the only friend I have right now," Norbert said. "Speaking of which, I too, have a secret."

Nuts sprang into her seat and stared excitedly at Norbert, her bright blue eyes wide as saucers. Norbert pulled a pink sheet of paper from his pocket.

"When I was looking for a screwdriver to fix the television, I found the address of the house that Baz knocked down last weekend. I was thinking one day we could..."

Before he could finish the sentence, Nuts scrambled into the hallway, knocking a school picture from the wall. She furiously clipped her crash helmet shut and wrestled her bike out of the front door.

"Let's GOOOO!" she shouted.

Chapter 17

"Good ideas are overrated."

Nuts only had one speed. GO. She rarely sat in the saddle, preferring to stand on the pedals with her hips smacking against the handlebars. The bike swung left to right so violently that Norbert felt sea sick.

He clung to the seat post and, with one eye open, stared up at the tower blocks and their cobweb of footbridges. Instead of heading out into the dark woodland surrounding the city, Nuts steered down a street lined with houses. Up ahead, Norbert saw sharp skyscrapers that pierced the clouds.

"That's the city centre," Nuts shouted. "The tallest one is Trixie's Tower. That's where my mum works."

"Are we going there?" Norbert shouted.

"No, we're going around it. The building where Baz found you is out in the woods, on the other side of the city."

The streets were empty but for the occasional bus, which belched plumes of black smoke. The kids held their breath as they overtook.

"Where are the cars?" Norbert asked.

"Nobody has cars, except for the high ups. And the Hawks," Nuts said.

The streets in between Nuts' district and the city centre swirled this way and that, with trees peppered along wide pavements. Every house was an identical concrete box, which looked to Norbert like a child's drawing. Two downstairs windows, two upstairs and a triangular roof. The only distinguishing features were the colour of the front door, and the state of the front garden.

Norbert noticed a particularly manicured lawn with colourful flowers that grabbed his attention from the top of the street. Nuts raced towards it with particular fervour.

"What are you doing?" Norbert screamed.

She hopped up the kerb and into the lawn, digging a trench in a bed of purple azaleas and smashing through a wooden sign advertising Shadow Runners.

"Anna's house," Nuts said, looking this way and that to check she had not been seen.

"We've got two hours before Mum gets home, which means we don't have long here," Nuts whispered.

She leaned her bike against a tree and the kids nervously left the shadows to approach the tall iron gates. The words PUZZLE MANOR were welded into vertical spears, and a heavy metal chain looped between them. Nuts stood guard while Norbert inserted the key into the padlock.

"Are you sure this is a good idea?" he asked.

"Good ideas are overrated," she said.

Norbert noticed that her voice sounded hollow and scratchy. It was the first time he had seen her get nervous. Her hands shook a little as she unlooped the chain, and the two kids slipped through the gap.

As they walked up the driveway, they were hit by the smell of bonfire. Despite the snow and rain of the last couple of days, the mountain of rubble still poured off wisps of smoke. White stone columns lay shattered. Piles of bricks were scattered among charred beams.

"Do you recognise anything?" Nuts asked.

Norbert shook his head.

"The gates? The name Puzzle Manor?" she pressed.

"No. I'm sure I've never been here before. I mean, apart from when you and Baz found me, of course."

They picked their across jagged slabs of brickwork. Norbert crouched down and inspected a bundle of cables.

"These are very big, for a house," he said.

"It was a big house," Nuts said.

"Nuts, cables in your home are as wide as your finger, at most. These are as big as my arm. You would expect to see something like this in a factory or some place that needs a massive amount of power."

"Perhaps she had televisions in every room," Nuts suggested. "Living the dream."

Norbert shook his head.

The sound of a car engine rumbled in the distance, and Nuts grabbed Norbert's sleeve.

"Run!" she shouted.

They scrambled across the mountain of sharp rubble and dropped down into a cavity just about big enough for the two of them. Plasterboard walls were crumpled around them like a smashed cardboard box. Norbert twisted to avoid being cut by a cracked mirror which hung over the remnants of a sink. Fragments of a porcelain toilet threatened to pierce the soles of their shoes. Nuts and Norbert held their breath and listened to the vehicle approaching the building site.

A car door slammed shut and the kids heard footsteps clambering onto the gravel.

"They know we're here," Norbert whispered. "They must have found your bike."

Nuts put her finger to her lips. She pulled a loose shard of broken mirror from the wall and lifted it slowly until she could make out the reflection of a figure.

A woman stood on the edge of the wreckage. Nuts dropped the mirror, and it smashed.

"It's Tr...Tr..." she mouthed. "It's Trixie!"

"Is someone there?" the woman called out, her playful voice echoing across the jagged mountain.

The kids held their breath, sinking ever deeper into the pit in which they hid. Norbert lifted a second piece of glass from the floor, nervously raising it until he caught Trixie's reflection. She wore a long, scarlet coat, patterned in what looked like snakeskin, and had an explosion of curly blonde hair.

Nuts tucked her head alongside Norbert's and they watched Trixie peer around the site before pulling a smartphone from her pocket. Nuts put a hand over her mouth to silence her gasp.

"As you can see," Trixie began, holding the phone at arm's length and speaking into the screen. "Puzzle Manor is gone. Kaput. A very unfortunate fire reduced it to rubble. So there is really nothing more to discuss. Your bizarre campaign is embarrassing, and quite irritating. It ends, now. Don't contact me again, Connor."

Norbert narrowed his eyes.

"What did you two get up to today?" Kara asked.

"Homework," Nuts said, her face still red from the exhausting cycle home.

Kara shook her head.

"Now I know you're lying. What did you really do? Norbert, did you go out?"

Nuts shot Norbert a look that sent shivers down his spine. Kara, too, stared at him with daggers in her eyes. He set down his spoon into his empty soup bowl and responded, carefully.

"I don't have a home, so I suppose I'm always out. So in that sense, yes, I went out."

Kara scooped up the crockery and shoved it by the sink.

"You two better not be getting in trouble. You know what happened to Sari's kid?"

"Sari has a kid?" Nuts said.

"Exactly."

Kara cocked her head back and made a *pff* noise, to indicate something disappearing into thin air.

"What happened to her kid?" Norbert asked.

"We don't ask questions, Norbert. But whatever it was, I don't want it happening to you. Either of you. I searched and searched the missing persons records today and there's nothing for you, going back years. That is not right, Norbert. Why didn't your parents call the police and report you?"

Norbert looked up at Kara with a sad smile.

"I told you. They..."

She made a *pff* noise, and he nodded.

"How come it's not attached to the wall?" Nuts asked. She poked her head out of the bedroom door to check her mum was still washing up, and not eavesdropping.

"It has a battery to power it, and it communicates with satellites," Norbert said. "It's wireless. She was filming a video."

"It can film video?" she said, eyes scrunched up in disbelief. "But it's like, *that* big."

Nuts pinched her fingers together.

"Yes. It's a television, camera, map, all rolled into one. But that's not the weird thing. The weird thing is that you *don't* have one," Norbert said.

"Err, maybe because I'm not the most important person on earth? The saviour of the entire world? Trixie was the world's youngest billionaire. She's an amazing inventor. She is bound to have a magic phone."

Norbert laughed.

"Where I'm from, everyone has one. Children as young as five have one. They're practically free."

"So you're from the future, then," Nuts said. "You must be."

Norbert shook his head.

"Time travel is impossible, Nuts."

"Could be possible for you," she said. "You're a genius. You know all this stuff about satellites and electronics. Maybe you invented a time machine but you don't know it, because you haven't invented it yet."

Norbert pondered this, but it made no sense. He was certain that if he had built a time machine, he would remember.

"I have to get home. Baz is expecting me to be back," he said. "But there's one thing that really bothers me more than the smartphone."

Nuts raised her eyebrows.

"*Connor*," Norbert said. "Trixie was making that video for Connor. That's my dad's name."

Nuts shrugged. "Is it rare?"

"No, I suppose not."

Chapter 18

"How is that to do with a moth?"

B az shouted "Who is it?", before cracking the door just enough to peek through the gap. He opened it up and thrust his head outside, looking up and down the gangway before hustling Norbert inside. His eyes were wide and sweat glistened on his forehead.

"Norbert...the...the television. What did you do?!" he stammered.

"I fixed it. Is it working okay?"

Norbert followed Baz into the lounge, starting to feel like he had made a mistake by interfering with Baz's belongings. He had only meant to help, but Baz seemed rattled by it.

"A moth had got inside it," Norbert explained. "I had to use a fuse out of the iron. It was either TV or pressed clothes. I hope that's okay."

The pair walked into the lounge where a weather forecast blared out for Puzzle Forest. A woman stood by a model of the walled city and said it was only three weeks until Shadow Runners, and the outlook was cold but dry.

"It works," Norbert said. "That's good, isn't it?"

Baz held up his remote control, on which were two pairs of rubbery buttons shaped like triangles, some pointing up, some pointing down.

"For eight years I've had this television, and these buttons do the volume. These ones do nothing. Until today."

Baz darted back down the hallway and pressed his ear to the front door. Satisfied there were no footsteps outside, he returned to the lounge and jabbed the up arrow. The television screen changed to a vast arena with crowds chanting. On the sandy ground stood a mechanised animal, as big as a car. As it swung its paws, they could see a person inside it, controlling the machine with levers. Norbert sat next to Baz, who was still standing, hypnotised by the screen.

"It's a sport, Norbert. There are two of these metal creatures, like diggers. They are warming up, but I think they're going to fight. It's called Beast Battle."

"Okay," said Norbert, taking it in. "Baz, you seem a bit freaked out. What's up? Is this sport not normally on."

Baz stared at Norbert, his eyes wide and intense. "Absolutely not. What is it? Where is it happening? *When* is it happening? Norbert, if we get busted having this on our TV, we're...done. I'm serious."

Norbert thought for a moment, and he remembered the cable tie which he had snipped through. He explained to Baz as best he could.

"Do you know how television works? Roughly speaking."

"Well, I assume the pictures come through that cable that runs into the wall there." offered Baz. He sat down beside Norbert.

"No, that's the power cable. The images and sound come through waves in the air. Like a radio."

"You what? Invisible waves?" asked Baz. "I really want to understand it. I was thirteen when we moved to Puzzle Forest so I never learned. Can you explain it, Norbert?"

"When I talk to you, the sound travels in a wave from me to you. My mouth vibrates the air in a certain way, and that wave travels to your ears, which decode it. Got that?"

Baz nodded.

"Well TV and radio work in a similar way. Something broadcasts a wave, and it travels into your house and then your TV antenna - like your ears - picks up the wave and decodes it into pictures and sound."

Baz stared down at the coffee table, concentrating hard on Norbert's explanation. "So why can't we hear the TV shows with our own ears, even when it's turned off."

"They're a different wavelength and your ears can't tune into them."

"Okay, so how is that to do with a moth?"

"Nothing, Baz. Your TV broke because of a moth, but while I was inside,

I found a cable tie limiting what it could listen out for, and I got rid of it. So now the television is no longer locked to the official Puzzle Forest channel. Have you tried looking for others?"

"Yes," Baz said. The only new one that works is number nine, the sport I showed you. All the rest are white fuzz right up to 99, then it goes back to the official channel."

He flicked back to the mechanised sport. A new character appeared, and began to warm up. It looked like a dragon made of car parts.

"So where is this event taking place?" Baz asked. "It looks like the future. Can waves travel back in time?"

Norbert chuckled, then realised Baz was not joking and immediately stopped.

"Perhaps it was recorded before Puzzle Forest existed and is now being broadcast?" Norbert suggested.

The two of them watched the Beast Battle. Baz sat mesmerised, barely able to blink.

"If there was a sports pitch that big in the city, I would know about it. My job takes me all over the city."

"Someone must be broadcasting it, right now." Norbert said. "But why would they broadcast a sport across the city, but then hack everyone's television to not be able to tune into it?"

With that, they both slumped back into the sofa, their brains exhausted from thinking.

"How was your day? I forgot to ask," Baz said.

Norbert thought back to hiding in the wreckage of Puzzle Manor, watching Trixie record a video on a smartphone. He wasn't a great liar, but had to do his best.

"Me and Nuts played dominos," he said.

Baz nodded. He spoke quietly, as if there might be people listening from the kitchen.

"Norbert, I appreciate you fixing the TV. You know that if we get busted for unlocking this channel, *and* I'm harbouring an unknown person, we'll both be taken away and never seen again?"

Norbert's eyes widened and he sat up nervously. "Shall I put the cable tie back in?"

Baz exhaled slowly, rubbing the tension from the back of his neck.

"No. Let me watch it a little bit longer. It's like a window into the future."

Chapter 19

"The radiation killed him."

"Nuts, if you don't mind me asking, what happened to your dad?" Norbert asked.

The two walked side by side along a muddy trail which snaked through the tall pine trees.

"He walked out on us, when I was little," she said.

"I'm sorry," Norbert replied.

Nuts shrugged. "He was a bit like you. Didn't believe the radiation would kill him. Climbed the wall. The radiation killed him."

Norbert shuddered at the thought of her father disintegrating in the burning wilderness beyond the city walls. He thought of how naive he had been on that first night when he climbed the ladder, and was more grateful than ever that Baz had come to his rescue. The fact his street was missing from maps still perplexed him.

Half an hour after they had left Nuts' flat, they saw light between the tall trees. The forest opened up to reveal a vast, glistening. Nuts dumped her heavy backpack and extracted her wingsuit.

Norbert looked away as she changed, staring up at the towering trees that lined the shore.

"Can you pass me my crash helmet?" she asked.

He unclipped it from her rucksack and thumbed three deep gauges in the crown.

"Did you get in a fight with a bear?" he joked, tossing it to her.

"No, a staircase," she said, wrestling it onto her head.

She climbed a tree, racing up from branch to branch. Birds fled as Nuts hauled herself up to where the branches were as thin as a broom handles, and the whole thing weaved in the wind.

"How's this?" she shouted down to Norbert. He gulped.

"I don't want to say it's 'okay', because it's not," he called out carefully. "But I don't want you to climb higher either. Just, come down. It's too dangerous."

Between the tree trunk and the water was a sandy beach. If the wingsuit failed, Nuts would crash into the ground directly below the branch on which she was balanced. To make it to the water she would have to manoeuvre her body into a horizontal position and glide all the way over the beach. Norbert half covered his eyes.

Nuts looked out over the lake and with barely a second's hesitation, leaped away from the trunk. She spread her arms and legs into a star shape, pulling the fabric taut between her thighs and elbows. It all happened in a fraction of a second, but to Norbert, the image of his new friend falling slowed time.

He watched in horror as Nuts plummeted toward the ground. But as she picked up speed she began to drift away from the trunk towards the water. With just a few metres until impact, her wings billowed with air and she whooshed over the beach toward the lake, tumbling into the surface with an explosive splash. Norbert ran to the water's edge and saw Nuts resurface, gasping for breath.

"Woooo!" she shouted. "It works!"

The two of them lay on the sand, as they waited for Nuts' wingsuit to drip dry on the branch of a tree. She made Norbert recount, again and again, how she fell downwards like a capital J, vertical at first but then suddenly gliding sideways towards the lake.

"You know what this means?" she asked excitedly. "The first part of any fall will be downwards, but then when I get enough speed I'll glide. So the higher the better. I can do this. I can get my BASE number. I need to do a Building, Aerial, Span. I've now done the E for Earth."

Norbert forced a smile but it terrified him. He had already faced too much loss to watch Nuts hurling herself off a building. He turned his head to face away from his friend and looked out over the lake.

"Nuts, the day I woke up in the basement of that house, I was at the lake. Maybe it was this one. I had a plane that I had made."

"You made an aeroplane?" she interjected.

"Only a model. It was a replica of the one my parents were on when they went missing. I flew it at the lake, and it was a stormy day because I wanted to simulate the conditions of their crash. It hit the lake and split apart, and the tail section floated."

He skimmed a stone across the surface of the cold, still water.

"So it's possible they survived," Norbert continued. "They were in the tail, you see. And that morning, watching the video of the tailpiece floating on the lake, I felt hope. I could almost see them inside, fighting for survival. Coming home. Then the very next day I'm in this place and Carston City is burned to a crisp. No planes in the sky. Nothing. I'm further than ever from getting my family back together. I'm so, so lost."

His eyes reddened and tears formed in the corners. Nuts put her arm around his shoulder, soaking his hoodie with her wet hair.

"It's okay," she said. "We'll find them. Together."

Nuts twitched, and raised her head from his shoulder. With her wide blue eyes she peered right past Norbert, ducking her head left and right to get a better view.

"What is it?" he asked.

"That bush moved," she said.

In a flash of red hair Nuts bolted across the beach, kicking up sand and hurdling over fallen logs. Norbert heard a shriek as Nuts dived onto a bush, completely crushing it against the ground.

"Get off me!" came a shrill, familiar voice.

Nuts rolled off onto the sand and Anna staggered to her feet, spitting sand from her mouth. She plucked spears of bracken from her waistcoat and straightened her black bob.

"Why are you watching us?" Nuts said, jabbing a finger into Anna's chest.

"I was just enjoying a day at the lake," she said, backing away.

"With binoculars?"

"I birdwatch. The question is, what are *you* doing here?" Anna said, gathering momentum. She began to step toward Nuts, who, despite being taller, backed away.

"Who is this boy?"

"None of your business," Nuts said.

"I work for the city so everything is my business," she said.

Nuts sniggered.

"You are a girl scout who cosplays as an adult. You don't work for the city."

Anna gasped.

"I'm the cosplayer? You're the one dressed up as a butterfly, jumping out of a tree. You're lucky to be alive. I will be reporting you for..."

"For what?" Nuts asked, arms folded.

"Endangering your life. Unauthorised tree-climbing. Entering the woods without a permit. And most of all..."

She raised an arm toward Norbert. With one eye open she stared down the ridge of her index finger like the barrel of a gun.

"Him."

Chapter 20

"A for antenna."

"I'm sorry, Norbert. It's all I've got," Baz said, placing plates on the dining table in his tiny kitchen.

Parsnips had been cut into ghostly, pale chips, which sat alongside discs of carrot.

"It looks delicious, Baz. Thank you," Norbert said.

He shuffled the food around before preparing himself for the first bite.

"It's my fault. I've been eating all of your food. I'm sorry. I would like to chip in but I don't have my bank card."

Baz raised his eyebrows.

"You know, money," Norbert said.

"Oh. Right. Yeah we don't have that here. We get an allowance for essentials. My food is available tomorrow."

"Do you get to choose what you order?" Norbert asked, crunching some pepper onto the carrots.

Baz shook his head. "We're grateful for what we get." He lowered his voice before asking the next question. "Beast Battle?" he whispered.

Norbert shrugged. Having wedged a chair under the latch for the front door, Baz turned the volume down low and switched to channel nine.

A stadium packed with fans cheered a mechanical lion as it loped into the sandy arena. Covered with wires and pipes, the animal stood as tall as a telephone box, and had polished-chrome fangs. A second enormous robot stomped into the battlefield, shaped like a rhinoceros with a chainsaw where its horn should be.

Norbert's cutlery clattered onto his plate. "I have to keep reminding myself it's only robots," he said.

"Still, shall we watch something else?" Baz said. "This is a bit...savage, isn't it?"

Norbert nodded. "I don't like seeing the components getting destroyed."

Back on the official Puzzle Forest channel, a documentary showed the aftermath of the great radiation leak. A city burned and the sky glowed orange.

"Baz, how can you be certain that the Beast Battle isn't taking place inside Puzzle Forest? It's a big city," Norbert said.

Baz shook his head.

"No way, son. I've been down every street in this city at some point or another. I watch television every day. I read the paper. There is no way there's a secret stadium in here that I don't know about."

"Okay. And it can't be from the future, so it must be from the past, or outside the walls."

"Norbert, how many times do I have to say? There is nothing outside the walls. You saw those images? The world is destroyed."

Norbert nodded. He offered a few leftover parsnips to Baz, who took them gratefully.

"Baz, you know when you do demolition for your job? Could you begin to save me the electronics?" Norbert asked.

"What for? So you can fix them?" Baz replied.

"Well, most electronics are the same components; resistors, batteries, wires, capacitors, and so on. If I gradually build up a collection of parts, I can make things. Also do you know anyone with a soldering iron I could borrow?"

"What is that?" Baz asked.

"A tool with a hot tip. It melts metal which kind of glues electronic parts together."

"Nah. Every tool we have is accounted for. You get given it by the city if that's your job, and then when you finish that job or retire you give it back. If you lose a tool, there are serious consequences. My job doesn't use soldering irons, so I can't get one."

"But what if your hobby is electronics? Can't you buy one?"

"Ha. Hobbies are very strictly controlled. The city doesn't want people playing around with dangerous stuff. And you can't really buy things. You can make requests, and they grant you or they don't."

Baz leaned in and whispered "The city doesn't want you using your brain."

Norbert leaned in also, and whispered a reply. "How do they listen?"

"Nobody knows. But I don't like saying things against the city. That's what gets you disappeared." He sat back and spoke at normal volume.

"Sorry buddy, can't think how I can get a soldering iron I'm afraid. But I can start bringing you bits of broken toasters and stuff, if you like. We just toss it all in holes in the ground."

Norbert tried to sit in Nuts' room, then yelped in pain as his bottom connected with the floor. He sprang onto his knees and brushed the carpet until he found the culprit: a drawing pin. It was obvious where it had fallen from. One corner of a poster was flopped over, and Norbert smoothed it back flat.

It was an idealised painting of Puzzle Forest. Buildings sparkled in front of a purple sunset, and a huge antenna tower dominated the scene. Beams of white light scattered from its tip and in a friendly hand-written font it said "Get all your news from TRIXIE BROADCASTING CORPORATION". In mid air, having presumably leapt from the tower, was a scrawled image of a tiny flying human. Norbert pushed the drawing pin back in place.

"I'm going to jump it. Get my A for BASE." said Nuts, putting her hand on Norbert's shoulder. "A for antenna."

"Do you have to? I mean, can't we put a television outside and you jump off that antenna instead?" Norbert pleaded. "At the very least, ask your mum to make a new one with bigger wings. Way, way bigger wings. What do you tell her it's for, by the way?"

"Fancy dress," Nuts replied.

They both laughed, and Nuts lay back on her bed, tossing a book from foot to foot. Norbert asked if she knew any electricians, and explained that he wanted a tool to make electronic equipment.

"The only electrician I know is Anna's mum."

Nuts shook her head, as if hoping to flick the idea of Anna from her mind. The book landed heavily on her face.

Norbert asked, "Why do you hate Anna so much?"

Nuts sprang forward and stared at him with her electric blue eyes. He gulped, already regretting his question. The mere mention of Anna made Nuts boil with anger.

"She used to be in our gang, a few years ago. Bit of a do-gooder. She'd make us leave the den really early for lunch. Would tut if we took food from the canteen to eat later. It was like hanging out with a grown-up. 'Don't jump off that!' 'Put that fire out.' Then she joined Trixie's Little Helpers, and she got even worse."

Norbert cocked his head and half-closed his eyes. Nuts explained.

"Trixie's Little Helpers is a club on Thursday evenings for kids who wish they were Hawks. They get badges for doing achievements. Like, to get your *Cook* badge you have to help out at the canteen for a week."

"It doesn't sound so bad," said Norbert. "Why don't you go?"

"I did go, when Anna first started. But gradually, the achievements became meaner and more secretive, until they were straight up spying. Like to get your *Good Worker* badge you have to identify three people who are late for work. Literally stand outside an office in the city and make a note of who comes in at three minutes past nine. Then they get in real trouble. I left when they asked me to find three kids who were out after curfew, and report them. But Anna loved it, and by the time I left with one badge, her shirt was covered."

"She likes it. You don't. Why are you so angry with her?" Norbert asked.

"After I quit, Anna continued to be in the gang for a bit. We had a sweet den in the woods, with log chairs and balance beams. It had a roof which kept out at least half the rain, and a television made of sticks. It was brilliant. One day our den had been levelled. Looked like a ploughed field. And guess who comes to school the next day with a new badge. *Protector of the Woods.*"

"You think she told them about the den, just to get the badge?"

"Yep." Nuts said confidently. "I think she probably knew while we were building it that she planned to turn us in. So after that I stopped calling for her, and we built new dens in a different part of the forest. We haven't seen her since except at lunch when she's there with with her senior Trixie's Little Helpers cravat on."

"What's a cravat?" Norbert asked.

"It's a scarf thing. When I sit behind her at school I have to grip my chair to stop myself from yanking it tight around her neck and strangling her."

Norbert raised his eyebrows.

"And now she's on your case, Norbert. It's not good."

Chapter 21

"I might be a master criminal."

The following day, the streets were wet and mud splashed up Norbert's back as they rode. After weaving through the grubby, angular suburbs, the bike skidded to a halt. Norbert pulled his hoodie around to see a streak of mud splatter that ran all the way up his back.

"I'm soaked," Norbert said. "What happened to the mudguard?"

"It looked stupid. Anyway, I've got a little surprise."

Nuts leaned her bike against a tree and looked up and down the street. To Norbert, it looked indistinguishable from any other, with a cookie-cutter row of boxy grey houses tucked behind white picket fences.

Nuts ran up a garden path and scrambled over a fence.

"Come on!" she said.

Norbert reluctantly followed, dropping down into a neatly kept garden.

With an incredible burst of speed, Nuts ran up against the house and grabbed onto a window ledge. She hauled her head inside, and eventually wriggled through like a worm. Seconds later, the back door opened and her arm came jutting out, yanking Norbert into the house.

It smelled of dried flowers, which Norbert found quite calming, but Nuts held her nose in protest. She pointed up at a toolbox on a shelf.

"You wanted a soldering iron? Find it!" Nuts said, staring madly into Norbert's wide eyes.

"Is this Anna's house?!"

"Yes. And those are her mum's tools. Quick, she's dropping Anna off at a piano lesson, and she'll be back very soon."

"We can't steal her soldering iron!" Norbert said, in a half whisper. "This is burglary! Nuts, you've finally gone completely....nuts!"

"Just grab it! Go on. Is it that thing with the red handle?" Nuts said urgently, plunging a hand into the toolbox.

"That? That's a screwdriver. Seriously. It's that thing with a yellow handle and a cable. And the tube of wire next to it is the solder."

No sooner had he said it than Nuts had ripped the items from the box and stuffed them into her waistband. At that moment, Norbert saw a silhouette appear in the frosted glass of the front door. The two of them froze in horror as they heard a key slide into the front door.

Nuts and Norbert raced out of the back door, kicking it shut just as the front door swung open. The two burglars crept alongside the fence and scrambled over the back gate.

Back in Nuts' bedroom, she inspected the soldering iron, pointing like a magic wand.

"Show me how it works," she asked, but Norbert shook his head.

"Come on. You wanted a soldering iron, I got you one. What are you going to make with it?"

"Nuts, please! I'm already here in Puzzle Forest illegally, and now I'm a criminal. I don't want it. We have to take it back to Anna's house. We can post it through the letterbox tonight and she'll just think she dropped it on the doormat accidentally."

"No way. This is yours. My gift to you. I stole it, not you. To return to the scene of the crime would be madness."

"Well can we please keep it here?" asked Norbert. "I can't drag Baz into this."

"No problemo. My mum gave up tidying my room many years ago, as you can tell. We can keep a special little electronics stash under here."

Nuts grabbed a cardboard box from under the bed and lifted out a doll, which had drawing pins stuck in it and a little neck tie made of toilet paper.

She flung it across the room and handed the box to Norbert, along with the soldering iron and solder.

"Thanks Nuts." he said, feeling flush with emotion. "That's really kind of you. I mean, I never would have mentioned it if I'd have known we'd steal it, but it's very thoughtful of you. I don't think anyone's ever done a burglary for me before."

"Well, you say that, but you have some major gaps in your memory."

"True." Norbert laughed. "I might be a master criminal."

Chapter 22

"Frazzled like bacon."

Sprawled out on Nuts' bedroom floor, Norbert used the soldering iron to connect tiny pieces of circuitry. Wisps of smoke rose from the burning hot tip and the room smelled of strange chemicals as he worked.

"What are you making?" Nuts pleaded. "Why won't you tell me?"

Her suspicions had grown over several days, as the space under her bed filled with broken light switches and radios that Baz had smuggled home. Norbert's project related to Baz's television, and he was under strict instructions to keep that a secret.

"I told you about my BASE jump. You have to tell me what you're making," she said.

Norbert figured he could tell her some of the story, and just not mention the Beast Battle.

"Okay but you have to promise me you'll never tell anyone," Norbert said, putting down his tools and turning off the soldering iron at the wall.

"Of course I promise!" Nuts said, excitedly. She sat on the bed with wide eyes.

"Okay," Norbert began. "You know how televisions pick up signals through the antenna on top?"

"Nope."

"Televisions contain an antenna - think of it like a signal catcher - that catches these invisible waves floating through the air."

He pointed to the poster with Trixie's Broadcasting Corporation tower. It had little white lines, like flashes of lightning, pulsating from the top.

"These lines. These are meant to be the waves of information flowing through the air. And the television translates these waves into pictures, and puts them on the screen."

"And?" she said, impatiently.

"I'm making a device that will tell us where the television signal is strongest."

Nuts made him repeat it, and as the reality soaked in, she slumped back on her bed.

"You're making a television signal tester? You are RUBBISH."

"I want to find where the television signal comes from," Norbert said patiently.

Nuts jumped off her bed and flying-kicked the poster of the antenna, causing the wall to crack behind it. The downstairs neighbour banged on the ceiling and shouted. Norbert gathered his electronics protectively, sliding the box back under the bed.

"The antenna!" she said, nursing her foot. "Look, it's right there. You can practically see it from my window. That's where the TV signal comes from."

Nuts leaned against the bed and shook her mass of fiery red hair.

"Of all the things you could have made," she said. "I thought it might be a laser yoyo that could cut through a table. Or a magic box that you put dirty plates in and they come out clean. Even a robot owl would have been cool. But no. You built...a *measurer*."

Nuts went to the kitchen, tutting and muttering the whole way. She swigged some milk straight from the bottle and returned to his bedroom to find Norbert crouched over the smoking soldering iron, busily resuming work on his project.

"Did you not hear me, Norbert? We know where the signal comes from. Case closed. Make something else. Something dangerous. Something FUN!"

"You might be right. But what if the signal doesn't come from the antenna? What if it comes from another source? That's my hypothesis."

Nuts mouthed the word *hippopotamus*, eyes wide and head bobbing. Norbert continued to work, ignoring her growing irritation.

"If we discover there are signals coming from outside of the city walls," he said. "Then we've made the biggest discovery in the history of Puzzle

Forest. Imagine that we discover there is life outside these walls? I'll be one step closer to home. To Owly."

Nuts kicked the box of Norbert's electronic supplies, showering the carpet with components.

"Stop!" he said, scrabbling around the carpet to collect them up. The soldering iron melted a hole in the carpet.

"*Shut up* about outside, Norbert!" Nuts said. "There *is* no outside. How many times do me or Baz or Billy the Carrot have to tell you? The world is on FIRE. The owl. The plane. It's all nonsense. No planes have taken off in our lifetimes."

Norbert unplugged the soldering iron and wrapped the cable around the handle. He took it to the kitchen and ran it under the cold tap to cool it, which Nuts immediately shut off.

"It's not your water," she said, coldly.

Norbert shook his head.

"I have to try, Nuts. My home is out there somewhere, and I have to find it. It has a dishwasher too, by the way. And it's not magic."

"And I suppose it's so awful hanging out with me that you'd rather do science homework that a teacher hasn't even set! You're the worst friend, Norbert. Ungrateful."

"I'm not ungrateful," he said. Norbert returned to Nuts' bedroom and collected his newly-completed signal gun. It consisted of a wooden handle covered in colourful wires and lights, with the metal cup from an egg poacher on the front. Nuts sniggered when she saw it.

"I didn't do anything wrong," he said.

"You didn't do anything right."

Nuts held her bedroom door open and ushered him out. He kicked on the shoes he had borrowed days ago from her, his heels squishing down the backs as she herded him to the door.

"They're mine," Nuts said, kicking her trainers away from his feet.

Norbert paused on the doormat and looked at the wet concrete outside Nuts' door.

"Why don't you come with me?" he said.

Nuts shoved him out of the door in his socks, which immediately soaked through.

"Please, Nuts. At least let me take your shoes. I'll bring them back. I have miles to walk."

Nuts reluctantly kicked the old shoes across the threshold. The second one spun under the metal railing and sailed off the balcony to the street below.

"There. Now go!" she said. "Just disappear, like my dad did. Over the wall of death. And when you get frazzled like bacon don't say I didn't warn you. You're dumb, Norbert. The dumbest smart person I've ever met."

The door slammed shut.

Chapter 23

"Let's talk about the television."

B az returned from work one day to find his front door was already open. He looked down at the street below and gulped when he saw the roof of a police car. As he hovered on the walkway outside his flat, key in hand, a voice came from within.

"Come inside, Barry. We have some questions for you."

Baz thought about running but knew it was too late. He felt sick with nerves as he entered his flat. In the lounge sat two Hawks, one on each of his armchairs. They did not look round to see him enter the room, but kept their focus on the television, which showed a Beast Battle with the sound off.

One of the Hawks tapped the sofa cushion next to her a couple of times, but the gap looked uncomfortably narrow and Baz sat on the floor next to the television. He reached back to unplug it from the wall, desperate to make the illegal show go away.

"Leave it!" one of the Hawks commanded, sitting forward on the armchair.

She wore a long blue-grey coat and black boots, spattered with mud and snow. Her hair was cropped in a neat bob under a peaked hat which hung over her face like a beak. The Hawk logo embroidered on its side had oversized, all-seeing eyes, and talons big enough to heave a person into the air.

"Barry we have information that a boy has been frequenting this house.

Who is this boy?"

A bead of sweat ran down Baz's neck.

"He's just a friend," he stammered. "He pops over sometimes."

The Hawk, who went by number 434, withdrew a notepad and pen from inside her jacket and began to write notes.

"More than just 'sometimes', wouldn't you say?"

The other Hawk, who had folded her jacket over the arm of the sofa, wore a blue shirt with epaulettes on the shoulders. The Hawk's clothes were made of just the same cotton as Baz's tired overalls, but the addition of the logo seemed to turn their clothing into armour. This one went by number 813. Baz shook with fear as they conversed.

"Indeed. More than just the occasional visit from a friend. I don't like liars, do you 434?"

434 shuddered, returning to her notepad. "So what is the name of this friend of yours?"

"Norbert. His name is Norbert." Baz stammered, staring at the floor.

"And how old is Norbert? We heard he was a child." said 434.

"I heard that too," the second Hawk added.

The two women leaned forward, the peaks of their caps pointing menacingly down at Baz, like birds of prey cornering a mouse.

"Yes, I'd guess about twelve or thirteen," Baz said.

434 made a note of this information in her pad, and continued.

"So what's a grown man doing making friends with a boy? An unusual friendship, wouldn't you say Barry?"

Baz did not respond. He desperately wanted to run out of the door, but knew the Hawks would catch him quickly, and permanently.

"Let's talk about the television," said 813. "We turned on the television and you can imagine our surprise when we found this unusual television program. There is a city approved channel which our leader provides, and you are free to watch without restriction. This is not it. What is your explanation for this?"

On the screen, a mechanical dragon paced around a dusty arena, fire blasting from its mouth. A terrified man was shoved into the ring with it, armed with a small stick. Baz feigned shock, raising his eyebrows and gasping.

"I've never seen it before. My television must be broken."

434 cocked her head.

"You do surprise me, Barry. I think there's a thumbprint on the number nine button. What do you think, Blathnaid?"

The second Hawk glared at 434.

"I mean, 813. What do you think, 813?"

They passed the remote control between them and held it up to their eyes, studying the greasy print on the rubber button.

"It looks tapped to me," 813 said. "The man lies."

The two Hawks stood up, their silhouettes blocking the light from the hallway. Baz cowered, shaking his head.

"We need you to come with us, Barry."

434 withdrew a purple stick from inside her long coat. It had two sharp teeth protruding from one end, like a forked tongue, which crackled with electricity. Baz gripped onto tufts in the carpet and began to sob.

"Please don't take me," he begged. "I haven't seen that channel. My television is broken. I haven't done anything wrong."

As Baz was marched down the corridor outside his flat, tears rolled down his cheeks.

"I left my door open," he said. "Can we go back?"

434 sniggered as she prodded the lift button with her stick.

"Leave it ready for the next owner," she said.

Chapter 24

"You'll get your dumb badge."

"Okay, okay, wait!" Kara called sleepily, despite knowing the telephone could not hear her pleas. The ringing continued as she slid on her slippers and shuffled into the kitchen to answer it.

"Who is this? It's six in the morning," she said, her voice groggy and tired.

"Is that Kara?"

"Yes. Who is this?"

"I work for the crime prevention unit. Is Norbert at your house?"

The word *Norbert* was like an ice cube running down the back of her neck. She knew there was no point playing dumb.

"I don't think so. Let me double check in my daughter's room," she said.

Kara placed the phone on the worktop and burst into Nuts' bedroom without knocking.

"Have you seen Norbert? It's six in the morning and the Hawks are calling. I don't like it Nuts. Not one bit!"

Nuts shook her head and sat up, then followed Kara to the kitchen.

"No. He's not here," Kara said.

The phone was quiet for a moment. The two of them squeezed their ears closer to the receiver and were able to pick out the faint sound of typewriter keys in the Hawk's office.

"Nutella Greenwood, where is Norbert?" the Hawk asked.

"I don't know," she replied.

"If you see or hear from Norbert, call me at this number. Ask for detective 813. Have you written it down?"

Kara scribbled it on an envelope. The Hawk continued.

"Let me be clear, Nutella. This boy is wanted. If you harbour the boy at your house it is a criminal offence and you too, will be wanted. If you withhold information that could lead to the location of this boy, that is also a criminal offence. Please relay that to your mother. Is that clear."

"Clear." Nuts gulped. "...and excuse me?"

"What?"

"What is Norbert wanted for? What has he done wrong?"

"Don't ask questions," said the Hawk, who promptly hung up.

Kara paced back and forth in her kitchen, biting her nails.

"I can't believe you spoke back to that Hawk," she said. "What were you thinking?"

Nuts shrugged. She sat at the table with her head in her hands.

"I was just wondering what he did wrong. They can't arrest someone for no reason."

"Huh?" said Kara. "Of course they can! That's what they do. He could have done any number of things. Just the very fact he's not on the official Register of Residents is enough to get him arrested. And what about Baz? Whatever have they done to him? We should have turned in that boy the first day we met him."

Nuts looked out of the window, searching for police cars on the street and finding none.

"Mum, I'm going to cycle over to Baz's house and see if they're there. If I see any Hawks, I'll come straight back."

Kara, in a state of shock, nodded.

Twenty minutes later Nuts returned home, her mum swinging the front door open before she had a chance to knock.

"He's not there. The door was open. I rang the bell but nobody answered. Baz's bike is still outside."

"Oh my days!" exclaimed Kara. She spun round and put her hands on Nuts' cheeks. "They've taken him in. Nuts, I need you to promise me you won't get us tangled up in this. Promise me!"

"I promise Mum. It's okay. Baz didn't do anything wrong. Nor did

Norbert. If the problem is that Norbert's not on the register, can't they just add him?"

Kara faced away from Nuts and wiped a tear from her cheek with her forearm. She forced a smile, and looked at her daughter.

"Yes. I'm sure you're right, Nuts. Don't worry. Just leave the Hawks to do their job though. I don't want you and I getting another call from them about this. I've got to get ready for work now."

With her mum at work, Nuts pulled Norbert's electronics equipment from under the bed. Dozens of cereal boxes had been cut up and subdivided into neat compartments, each annotated with complex numbers and symbols. The soldering iron had its own box, the cord lovingly wrapped around the handle. But something was missing.

Nuts crawled under to make sure she hadn't missed anything, but came out empty-handed. The signal detector gun, which Norbert had spent hours and hours building, was gone.

"What would Norbert do?" Nuts said to herself.

The doorbell rang, and Nuts slid the box under the bed before opening the front door.

"Anna? What are you doing here?" Nuts asked.

The pleated tartan skirt of her school uniform snuck out beneath her puffy winter coat.

"I'm looking for the boy," she said, peering past Nuts, hoping for a glance of Norbert.

"He's not here. How do you even know he's missing?" Nuts asked, furiously.

"An alert went out this morning for Trixie's Little Helpers. We try to do our bit, you know. We want everyone to be safe."

Nuts grimaced.

"You want to find Norbert so you can call in the Hawks and collect your tattle-tale badge. Someone ends up getting disappeared but what do you care, because you've got something to sew onto your cravat. You are the worst, Anna."

Nuts swung the door shut, but it bounced off Anna's black leather shoe. The young visitor pushed her way in, catching Nuts off guard, and rushed through to the kitchen.

"Norbert?" Anna shouted.

Nuts grabbed Anna's jacket and pinned her against the wall.

"Don't pretend you're doing this out of the goodness of your heart," she sneered.

"Nuts, I do want to get my *Detective* badge," Anna admitted. "For that I have to provide a piece of critical information to the Hawks. So yes, you're right. But we can work together and both get what we want."

"I don't *want* the Hawks to find Norbert, so why would I help you?"

Anna grabbed Nuts' wrist and twisted it, freeing herself. She sat, panting, on a kitchen chair.

"Nuts, the Hawks will find Norbert in a matter of hours. That's what they do. They're unstoppable. With the greatest respect, you're not going to find him on your own. You're not exactly known for your brains. No offence."

"Firstly, just because you say 'no offence' doesn't mean you have a right to be offensive. Secondly, what's the point of finding him with you, if that means we immediately call in the Hawks and hand him over? I'll do this with my own stupid brain, thank you very much."

Nuts held open her front door and made a sweeping motion to usher her out. Anna defiantly went into the lounge, pulling back a curtain to look behind it, and then crouched to inspect the gap behind the sofa.

"I know you stole my mum's soldering iron. What did you want that for?" Anna asked.

"I don't know what you're talking about Anna. What's a *soldiering* iron?" Nuts asked, with deliberate mispronunciation.

"You know exactly what it is, and I know you stole it. In fact, I bet I know where it is."

With that, Anna sprang up from the sofa and burst into Nuts' bedroom. She knew her way around the flat, as they had been friends when they were small. In Nuts' messy bedroom she flung the cupboard doors open and looked inside, while Nuts watched nervously from the bedroom doorway.

"See? Nothing there. I didn't steal this *shouldering* iron of yours. So can you please leave now?" Nuts said, with her arms folded.

Anna gave up on searching the wardrobe and turned to leave, defeated. She walked back through the room, and kicked a ball in irritation. When it bounced straight back at her, she froze. Nuts fixed her with a gaze that said 'don't you dare', but it was too late. Anna dived to the floor and crawled under the bed. Nuts pulled her out by the ankles, and in Anna's hands was the cardboard box with the yellow-handled soldering iron.

"Aha! As I suspected. I'm going to tell the Hawks." she gloated, pointing the iron at Nuts.

"Anna, please," Nuts said, swiping at the tool. "They've taken Baz, don't make them take me too. Anyway it's your word against mine, I'll throw it in the river."

"Oh really and who do you think they'll believe? A known accomplice of a runaway, or the girl who is one badge away from being Senior Leader at Trixie's Little Helpers?"

She stood up, dusted herself off and walked out of the bedroom door with a smug grin.

"Okay wait, Anna," Nuts pleaded. "You want your *Detective* badge, right? I've got an idea."

Anna paused in the doorway of the flat, the cord of the soldering iron swinging by her knee.

"I'll help you find Norbert," Nuts continued. "Just promise to give me thirty minutes before you tell the Hawks. Just say it took that long to get to a phone. That gives me enough time to tell him that they've taken Baz, in case he doesn't already know that. You'll get your dumb badge for providing the information."

"Deal."

Chapter 25

"Cleanup needed."

On the messy carpet of Nuts' bedroom, she and Anna pored over Norbert's diagrams and electrical components.

"He's got some fascination with waves. Television waves, to be specific," Nuts said. "He doesn't seem to understand that the television signal comes from the antenna in District Four. For some reason he built a device to confirm what everyone knows."

Anna nodded, looking out of the window as she tried to process the information.

"But why? Suppose Trixie *does* have two antennas, one for backup, perhaps. Or one to reach people over the other side of Puzzle Forest. Who cares? Why would he be so obsessed with finding the source of the television signal?"

Nuts tried to recall the conversation she'd had with Norbert a few days ago, when she had rudely dismissed Norbert's invention as a waste of time.

"I think that he wants to rule out that there are any waves coming from outside the walls."

Anna laughed. "Oh, he's one of those. Does he think the Earth is flat, too?"

"Exactly, that's what I said!" Nuts said. The two girls shared a brief laugh, before recoiling at the awkwardness. Nuts slumped back against her wardrobe while Anna examined the poster on the wall, touching the lightning strikes bursting out of the antenna's tip.

"There must be some reason he's suspicious about the television signals," Anna said. "He was willing to burgle my house to figure it out.

When you went out and used this machine of his, what did it say?"

Nuts looked embarrassed and sighed.

"I didn't go. I thought it was a waste of time. We had a bit of an argument about it and he left."

"Okay so let's think about this," Anna said. "He's got a detector gun. A measurer of some sort, that tells him where TV signals are the strongest. He's presumably going around Puzzle Forest taking measurements, which he will then note down on a map."

"Should we go to Baz's house and see if we can find this map, or any more clues?" Nuts suggested. "The door was open when I went this morning."

"I don't like it, Nuts. I would need to ask for approval from my leader at Trixie's Little Helpers," Anna said.

Nuts kicked on her boots and stood in the doorway, ready to leave. Anna shook her head then followed, reluctantly.

Nuts pushed open the door to Baz's flat and the two girls slipped inside. Anna went to turn on a light, but Nuts batted her hand away.

"Keep them off. Neighbours will be on the lookout for signs of activity in here," she said.

The girls tip-toed from room to room to check there were no Hawks waiting inside the flat. In the lounge, they found a sheet had been hung from the ceiling to section off a little bedroom for Norbert. Three sofa cushions lay on the floor with a pillow and a neatly folded blanket.

They rooted around for signs of the map, but found nothing.

"Psst. Look at this." Nuts said, pointing to Baz's television. It was wrapped in tape which said WARNING DO NOT TOUCH.

"Okay, better not touch," Anna said, but before she could finish her sentence, Nuts was ripping the tape off.

"Can't you read! It'll make noise and the Hawks will hear," Anna said.

Nuts turned the volume down before the screen came to life, and the two of them watched in total amazement as the Beast Battle came on. A stadium flashed with lights, spectators pointed smart phones at a drone which swooped overhead. A gigantic screen at the back of the arena showed a countdown to an upcoming matchup, featuring a terrifying mechanical bear.

The girls slowly backed away from the screen, so mesmerised that Anna tripped over the coffee table and folded into a heap on the sofa. At no point did her eyes leave the chaotic images on the screen.

"Did you know about this? Well, I guess not," Anna concluded, as she watched the reflection of the television flicker on Nuts' wide, unblinking eyes.

Nuts grabbed the remote control and jabbed at the channel up button. The television cycled through screen after screen of grey fuzz. Eventually it returned to the standard Puzzle Forest information channel which showed a highly optimistic weather forecast. A man in a suit stood in front of a model of the city, holding a cardboard cloud. Nuts continued flicking and eventually returned to the Beast Battle, where a mechanical dinosaur breathed fire from its jaws.

The two girls sat side-by-side on the sofa, their faces pale. The gleaming technology, enormous stadium...even the presenter's clothes; Beast Battle felt like a window into a fictional world.

"So this is what Norbert was hunting for. The source of the weird channel," Anna said.

The two were snapped from their daze by noise outside the front door. Nuts stabbed the 'off' button on the remote and the two of them sprang up from the sofa. They saw light flood into the hallway and knew they could not make it to the kitchen without being spotted. Nuts grabbed Anna by the blazer and dragged her towards Baz's bedroom where they scrambled under the bed.

The girls watched three adults pass by the bedroom door, stomping purposefully toward the lounge. Two wore the standard black Hawk boots, which Anna dreamed would one day be hers. The third person went by in a flash of scarlet. The kids held their breath, terrified of getting found.

"This is the television in question," a voice said. A few seconds later the girls heard the excited Beast Battle commentary increase in volume, then suddenly go silent.

"I am very displeased at this. How did it happen?"

The female voice was familiar but taut with irritation. Under the dusty mattress, Anna and Nuts looked at each other in alarm.

"Trixie!" Anna mouthed, baring her teeth. They shuffled even deeper under the bed until Anna was squished against the wall. From their vantage point they could only see an empty slice of hallway, with a wonky picture of Puzzle Forest. Nuts assumed that Baz had knocked it, when he was dragged kicking and screaming from his apartment.

"We aren't sure," came a voice from the lounge. "We came to interview the man who lives in this flat about another matter, and turned on the television while we were waiting for him. We have never seen anything like it."

"And this man," Trixie said. "What do we know about his involvement? Does he have a criminal past?"

"He claims he's never seen this strange channel before. We took him in for questioning. He seems like a good citizen; works in demolition. The only thing we found on his file is that four years ago his wife was taken in for questioning. She has not returned."

"I see," said Trixie. "And what were you two here for? You said you came here to question the demolition worker about something else."

The second Hawk began to speak now.

"We had reports of a twelve to fourteen year old boy frequenting this flat. According to the informant, there is no record of this boy at all."

Nuts flashed a savage glance at Anna. The flat fell silent and the scarlet boots returned to the hallway, heels clicking on the uncarpeted concrete. The hideaways watched in horror as the boots stopped at the bedroom doorway and swung their sharp points to face them.

Anna and Nuts held their breath and watched Trixie's red snakeskin boots methodically work their way around Baz's bedroom. Drawers were opened, and closed, while the two Hawks watched from the doorway, their hands held neatly behind their hips.

"813 and 434, correct?" Trixie asked.

"Yes ma'am."

"Who else knows about the television. Did you tell anybody about this at headquarters since you discovered it this morning?"

"No ma'am," said 813, her voice dry and raspy. "We didn't file our report yet until we had all the facts."

"Very well."

BANG! A gunshot rang out, deafening the kids under the bed. In what felt like slow motion, the girls watched a Hawk collapse into the bedroom. Before her head had crashed into the carpet, another blast rang out. The second Hawk folded over in the hallway, her body limp.

With the noise ringing in their ears, Nuts and Anna stared at each other in disbelief. Trixie stepped over the bodies and picked up the phone in the hallway.

"This is Trixie. We have a cleanup needed at....[pause]...28589."

After a moment's pause, she continued.

"Oh, and the house has a television in the lounge which needs to be destroyed. Not fixed. Not turned on. Just destroyed. Is that clear?"

There was a click as Baz's telephone was returned to its hook, followed by the sound of the front door swinging shut. Finally, the girls were able to breathe again.

Chapter 26

"It didn't happen."

Nuts crawled out from under the bed and dusted herself off. She examined the fallen Hawks, toeing their bodies for signs of life.

"Come on," she said. "We have to get out of here before more Hawks come to clean up."

The room remained silent. Nuts reached under the bed, felt for the fur of Anna's hood and dragged her out onto the bedroom floor. Curled up in a foetal position with her eyes clamped shut, Anna looked shrivelled and ghostly.

"Anna, get up! Let's get out of here," Nuts said, toeing her into life with her canvas shoe.

She glanced out into the hallway and grimaced, putting her hand over her mouth.

"Don't look down," she said to Anna, who was staggering to her feet.

On the hallway floor, the dark uniforms lay still as shadows. Anna allowed herself just one glance to ensure she did not step on the bodies, then bolted out of the front door. Nuts crouched by the body, unconcerned by the distant wail of sirens. She prised a notepad from the stiff fingers of one of the Hawks, the plastic cover still warm to the touch.

Protruding from the Hawk's jacket was a red metal cylinder, which Nuts tried to draw out. The sirens were close now, and she heard the screech of brakes in the street far below. Eventually the object – like a broom handle as long as her forearm – popped free of its leather holster and Nuts stuffed it in her waistband. She raced out of the flat, head down across the gangway. The lift clunk into position and dinged. As the doors opened,

Nuts disappeared into the stairwell, where she slid down the bannister to avoid the sound of her footsteps.

In a bleak park at the base of Baz's tower block, she spotted Anna walking determinedly toward her suburb. Nuts ran to catch up.

"Where are you going?" she shouted, her breath ragged from running down fifty-eight flights of stairs.

"Home," Anna said without looking over her shoulder.

"But we have to find Norbert? Did you not see what I just saw? Trixie's a maniac! She just murdered two Hawks for no reason at all. Ordered a cleanup like someone had dropped a milkshake. She's going to disappear Norbert if she can find him. We have to find him first!"

Anna walked through a children's sand pit which she and Nuts had once played in. She tried to ignore Nuts and pushed aside a rusted swing, yanking her hood over her head to shut out the world.

"You can find him," Anna said. "I'm not sure I saw anything. I was under a bed, remember?"

Nuts grabbed Anna's shoulder to slow her, but the smaller girl wrenched it free and picked up her pace.

"What?" Nuts said. "What aren't you sure about? Trixie is a killer."

Anna stopped in her tracks and span to face Nuts. Her words misted in the cold air like a dragon's breath.

"Shut up! Right now!"

Anna looked back at the jungle of tower blocks and shuddered. "We're just kids. We were in the wrong place at the wrong time. Trixie is the giver of life. Look around you, Nuts. All of this is because of her. Do you think she'd..." Anna leaned right in close, terrified someone might hear her words "...*end* someone? Of course not. There must be another explanation."

"Like what? You heard a gun shot and stepped over a body."

"I don't know, Nuts. Just leave me alone," Anna said, setting off once again through the snowy path towards her house.

Nuts jogged alongside as Anna's tirade continued.

"When I woke up this morning, I was a good girl. I had my whole life planned out; be the best at school, complete Trixie's Little Helpers, get into Mini-Hawks, get a job working for her in the city. And one day I might be in the Inner Circle. It was all perfect. Then I made the mistake of hanging out with *you*, and now it's a mess. Well you know what? There are rules, and laws, and logic for a reason. It didn't happen. It couldn't have happened. I'm going back home and going back to bed. I'm waking up, and I'm starting again. And this time there will be no Nuts in my day. Go away!"

Nuts gave up the chase and brushed the water from a swing, which creaked on rusted chains. She watched Anna fight her way through a hole in the hedge which separated their estates. On Nuts' side, the tower blocks cast shadows so vast that the snow didn't melt all winter. On Anna's side, every house had a proud front lawn, and the adults worked in the upper floors of the city's office blocks. What they did up there, Nuts didn't know or care. But she knew that there were walls *inside* Puzzle Forest, too. They just weren't a mile high.

She returned to her flat and stared across to Baz's tower block through binoculars she had only ever used to search for her pet rat, Vermina. She knew that if the Hawks found her footprint or a single red hair, then she would be next. No questions would be asked. She would be quietly ushered into a car and disappeared beneath a mountain of secretive paperwork.

She had to find Norbert before it was too late, so she went to her bed to think. As she reclined, she felt a spike in her lower back and remembered the stun-stick she had stolen from the crime scene.

It was made of cold metal and painted red. Heavy, like a torch, but narrower and longer. A button on the handle could not be pressed until she flipped up a special safety catch. Presumably to prevent people electrocuting themselves while they lay on a bed. The other end of the handle had two little spikes coming out like the jaws of a giant ant. Nuts flipped the safety off and squeezed the button, causing a crackle of blue electricity to leap instantaneously between the tips of the jaws. She smiled and thought how cool Norbert would have found this device. She touched the tiny, sharp jaws, and wondered how the spark would feel. Before she could stop herself, she gently touched the red button.

"Yeeeeaaaooooowww!" she screamed.

Nuts flung the device across her bedroom and squeezed her hand. Through teary eyes, she examined her finger tip, which had two black scorch marks. She put it into her mouth and sucked the pain away.

Next, she examined the notepad, flicking past pages detailing petty thefts, kids out after curfew and minor gossip which she would read later. On the last page, she found the word *Norbert*.

Lines darted out from his name like spider legs, connected to Baz, Kara, Nuts and Puzzle Manor. No mention of Anna. Other words scrawled on the page included 'boy with gun' and, double-underlined, 'television'. A crudely drawn circle with four cross marks was labelled 'Possible sightings'. It wasn't a map with enough detail for Nuts to find Norbert, but it told her that he had covered some serious distance in the 48 hours he'd been missing. The crosses appeared to be roughly north, south, east and west of the city centre, where the built-up part of Puzzle Forest met the woodland surrounding it.

Nuts assumed that this is what had triggered the manhunt; a series of calls had been made about a boy pointing a strange, home-made gun into the air. She turned the page, but it was blank, save for a spot of blood which had soaked through the paper.

She turned back to the spider diagram.

"Today," she muttered to herself. Nuts flipped forward to the first blank page.

"Tomorrow. The next day. The day after that..."

She flipped through blank page after blank page, thinking about the unwritten life of Hawk 813. She thought of kids who might never know why Mummy didn't come home. She had heard of people disappearing, but never seen it. Never seen how fast and easily it happens. All because of a boy who asked the wrong questions.

Nuts flipped it shut and phoned Kara at work.

"What time are you home, Mum?" Nuts asked.

"Leaving now. Everything okay?"

Nuts listed carefully to the fuzzy silence between their sentences. Ever-so-faintly, amid the static, she heard a click, like a motor whirring.

"Everything's fine, Mum. Just a bit bored from being home all day. See you soon."

Chapter 27

"I'm not shaking your spitty hand."

Anna answered her door, then slammed it immediately again in Nuts'
face.

"Go away!" she shouted through a flipped up letterbox. "I've got
nothing to say to you."

"Anna, open up and let me in! You can't pretend nothing happened. We
both saw it."

The door swung open and an arm grabbed Nuts, yanking her into the
house with surprising strength.

"Do *not* talk like that, Nuts! We live in a nice neighbourhood. Shoes!"
Anna barked.

Nuts kicked off her trainers and slumped on the sofa. Anna's house
was almost colourless, as if the entire building had been dunked in bleach.
Creamy-white sofa. Creamy-white carpet. The only splashes of colour were
gold trophies and photographs of Anna being brilliant. A framed bowling
card in which she scored eight strikes. A photo of her holding a three-tiered
cake that was bigger than her head. Nuts recalled her last attempt at baking.
She gobbled up the raw dough while her mum popped out to borrow a
cookie cutter. Then her focus came back to that morning's events, which
cast a dark shadow over the memory.

"Anna, I need your help. We have to find Norbert."

"We? *You* need to find Norbert, maybe. The Hawks need to find
Norbert. I don't even know him. I told you; I'm not involved in this," she

said haughtily.

Nuts rested her feet on a glass coffee table. Anna lifted them, pinching the socks to avoid full contact, and dropped them back to the floor.

"It's too late for denial," Nuts said. "You were under the bed when Trixie killed two Hawks in cold blood. So stop pretending your life is just going to go on the same as before, with badges and photos and cakes."

Anna looked out of the window, then yanked the curtains shut at the front of the lounge.

"Maybe I wasn't there," she said. "Maybe we both imagined it. It couldn't have happened, Nuts. And if anybody asks, that's what I'm going to say. Now I want to move on with my day. With my life. So please leave. I have homework." She crossed her arms and stared at Nuts.

"Anna, listen carefully. What can you hear?"

"Nothing." Anna said, briefly massaging her already red ear.

"Except a faint ringing noise that won't go away, right?" Nuts said.

Anna huffed, and sat opposite Nuts.

"My ears are ringing from the gunshots, Anna, and so are yours. We didn't imagine it. I need to find Norbert before the Hawks do. And if the Hawks find me, I'll tell them the truth. We witnessed Trixie kill shoot two Hawks. You can deny it all you like but there will be strands of our hair all over that house, including under the bed."

Anna gasped. She clutched a cushion against her chest. "Are you threatening me?!"

"Yes. I've asked you politely. I've reasoned with you. Now I'm threatening you. I'll do whatever it takes to find Norbert, and I can't figure it out on my own. Now please. Help me!"

Anna flung the cushion down and stomped to the front door. Nuts expected her to open it, but instead she jammed on the bolt which secured it shut.

"I hate you, Nuts. Once we've found Norbert, you must promise me you'll leave me alone. You can't blackmail me about this forever."

"Okay, deal. And I hate you too."

Nuts spat on her hand and offered it to Anna, who recoiled in horror.

"I'll help you find that miscreant, Nuts. I'm not shaking your spitty hand. Gross."

Nuts wiped it on a cushion [gasp!] and reached into her backpack, from which she pulled out the notepad. Anna sat alongside and studied the diagram of Puzzle Forest, with crosses that indicated possible sightings.

"So we now know why Norbert was obsessed with the television signal," Nuts said. "He'd found a way to watch that mad show which isn't on the main channel."

Anna nodded.

"It feels weird calling it the 'main channel' doesn't it? I never even thought of calling it a channel, because it was as simple as turning on the TV and there's a show. But as soon as there's more than one, you need a name for it."

"Exactly!" said Nuts, her eyes widening with excitement. "And Norbert saw that and thought to himself...."

Her train of thought fizzled out, and she looked down at the map, dejected.

"What did he think? How did he go from seeing there was another channel, to building a measuring gun? If it was me, I would have made some popcorn."

Anna thought about this.

"Norbert knew that new channel must have a source. It's like he found a thread, and couldn't stop pulling at it to unravel it all."

Nuts thought back to the time when Norbert was in his bedroom soldering his measuring machine together.

"I remember now! He had a hunch that the source of the television signal might be from outside of Puzzle Forest. I guess he had promised Baz not to tell me about the Beast Battle, and I'm still mad at him about that."

Anna's face screwed up into a look of horror and ridicule.

"Life *outside* Puzzle Forest? That's a new one. Or rather, a really really *old* one. I thought he was meant to be smart?" she said.

"That's what I thought, and I told him he was stupid. But that's what he does; he has a theory and tries to prove it. A hippopotamus."

Anna was incredulous. "*Prove* it? What needs proving? There are literally two libraries full of books about this. Video footage of mutant animals. We KNOW what's outside. Radiation and death. Can't he read?"

"He can read the books. He just doesn't believe them. He also doesn't think Trixie discovered gravity."

At this point Anna laughed, but Nuts shook her head.

"So now, knowing what he wants to prove, and that he has been spotted at the north, east, south and west of the city. Where is he now?" Nuts passed her the notepad.

"I cannot believe you stole from a Hawk," Anna said, shaking her head in dismay.

"She didn't need it anymore," Nuts said, darkly. Anna shivered.

"He's taking a reading all the way around the city. If they're all the same, then the signal comes from the antenna. If they're different, then they must be coming from somewhere else. If that's the case, perhaps he would want to get really high up, to get above the trees and even the wall."

They both said in unison: "The antenna!"

With that, Nuts leapt up, grabbed her backpack and stuffed the notepad alongside her wingsuit, a squished sandwich and a stun gun. Anna looked wide-eyed in alarm.

"You're going to the antenna?" she asked.

"No. *We* are going to the antenna. Come on! We've got to find Norbert before they do. A deal's a deal, Anna."

Chapter 28

"We are watching you."

On separate bikes, the two kids pedalled furiously through the twisting streets of Puzzle Forest. The last exhausting climb took them up a steep wooded slope, where the antenna had been built at the highest point in the city. Trixie's videos proudly stated it was the tallest building on Earth, and even though Nuts had a poster of it on her wall, she was taken aback by its size.

Around the tower was a tall fence, plastered with warning signs saying 'Danger of Death' and, ominously, 'We Are Watching You'.

Anna leaned her bike against a tree.

"Bury it," Nuts said, covering her own bicycle with branches and leaves.

"I hate this," Anna said, who did as she was told but seemed reluctant to get her hands dirty.

Nuts peered up, shielding her eyes from the sun as she scrutinised the rungs and platforms. Staircases snaked up the tower's first stage, presumably to allow maintenance workers to ascend it. As it soared above the height of the forest canopy, the structure narrowed to little more than a ladder, which pierced the clouds above.

"I can't see anybody up there. Can you?"

Reluctantly, Anna came out from the trees and looked up.

"I can't either," she admitted. "But I can't really see much past the top of those stairs and that's barely half way up. If he was at the top, we wouldn't be able to see him."

"Wait!" Nuts called. "Look at that!"

Nuts led Anna into the clearing around the base of the tower. They crouched by a section of the barrier in which the wire mesh had been peeled up the ground to create a triangular hole. Nuts sized up her shoe against an indentation in the mud.

"Yes! It's his footprint," she said. "He borrowed my shoes."

Nuts crawled through the hole, shredding her top on the sharp wires.

"What are you waiting for? Let's go!" she yelled back to Anna.

"I'm done," Anna said. "I said I'd help you find him, and now you've found him. You have thirty minutes, starting now."

Nuts rattled the diamond-shaped mesh. "No! Don't give up now!"

"We are the lucky ones, Nuts. You can mess your own life up looking for that boy but you can't mess up mine. If anybody ever asks me, then I'll deny all knowledge of hearing those gunshots and you can argue all you want. Let's see who they believe."

Anna pushed back her shoulders and straightened her cravat so that the badges lay flat.

"Okay fine," said Nuts. "Just pass me my bag before you go. I can't reach it."

Anna dragged the huge yellow backpack and shoved it under the fence.

"What have you got in there?" she asked. "It weighs a ton."

At that moment they heard the buzz of a motorcycle, and froze.

"Come quickly!" said Nuts. She swung the backpack onto her shoulders and raced toward the base of the antenna. "Let's hide in the tower. If you leave now and go back towards the woods, they'll see you running."

The engine noise grew louder as the bike weaved up the path. With just seconds before it reached the clearing, Anna crawled through the fence and joined Nuts. The two girls raced up the stairs, switching direction at each platform as they zig-zagged up and up. After eight storeys they were level with the tops of the surrounding trees. They paused their ascent and the echo of their clanging footsteps died away.

"The motorcycle. I can't hear it anymore," Nuts said.

"Maybe it went away?" Anna said, optimistically.

They crouched on the freezing steel floor, concealed behind a hip-height wall. Nuts gingerly raised up to look out, and caught sight of their pursuer kicking the leaves from Anna's bicycle.

"That Hawk found your bike," Nuts said. She shook her head angrily.

"Why didn't you hide it better?"

"Why did you drag me into a giant climbing frame marked 'Danger of Death'? *That's* the bad thing. Not my bicycle, which, by the way, would have been safely tucked away in my shed if you hadn't RUINED MY LIFE."

The two girls watched the Hawk remove her crash helmet and make notes on a pad. Anna rested her head on her knees and wrapped her arms around her shins.

"That should have been me," she said. "With a motorbike and a Hawk pen and miscreants to arrest. And instead, I am the criminal!"

She swung a fist to hit Nuts, but missed and thumped the metal wall of their enclave. It rang out like a gong. The Hawk looked up at the tower, and Nuts dropped down out of sight.

"What did you do that for?" Nuts hissed.

The motorcycle engine fired up again.

"Maybe she's leaving," Anna said, cowering in a corner.

The engine grew louder, and Nuts took a peak over the railing to see the Hawk circling the perimeter.

"Let's go up!" she said. "While the Hawk isn't looking."

Nuts set off and Anna reluctantly followed. They flew up the next flights of stairs, the whine of the motorcycle fading away as they ascended out of earshot. On a floor marked forty, they ran out of stairs to climb. The only way to go higher was a ladder, which appeared to go on forever.

Nuts gingerly rose to look over the guardrail, and nudged Anna to join her. They gasped at the view.

For miles and miles was a dark green carpet of forest, punctured here and there by clutches of tower blocks. The lights of the skyscrapers in the city centre sparkled. Nuts crept around the platform to look at the city wall, which she had only ever seen at ground level.

"That's amazing," she said.

"What?" Anna replied, clutching her stomach. "It looks like the wall always does."

"Exactly. Don't you think it's crazy that we're this high up and still can't see the top of it? Let's go higher!"

"Why? No!" Anna said, turning away from the staggering view. "I feel sick already. I'm not here to do sightseeing."

"But Norbert might be up there. If he got this far, he'd have gone all the way. That's how his mind works. He wants accuracy in his data, he's always going on about that."

"Ugh, Norbert. Who even is this kid?" Anna whined. "Literally destroyed my entire reputation and everything I've worked for, over a boy who barely said one word to me."

At the halfway point where the girls had stopped, the structure was barely wider than a climbing frame and it swayed, dizzyingly, like a ship's mast.

Nuts climbed to her feet and set a hand on the first rung.

"The Hawk will be able to see us," Anna said. She remained in a foetal position, shivering on the cold floor.

"I don't care. I want to find Norbert," Nuts said.

Anna peered over the edge to find the Hawk staring back at her through gigantic binoculars.

"Wait for me!" she said.

Chapter 29

"You kidnapped me!"

Nuts raced up the ladder with Anna scrambling to keep up. A metallic clang deafened them.

"What was that?" Anna said, her eyes wide with terror.

"Gunshot!" Nuts called over her shoulder. "The Hawk must be shooting at us."

Nuts ascended through the next hole and hopped off the ladder. They huddled on a platform barely larger than a dining table, and the entire structure wobbled in the wind. The treetops beneath were merged into one swipe of inky green, and in the forest clearing, Nuts could barely make out a vehicle, let alone a Hawk. Another gunshot rattled off, making a deafening ping as it struck the tower beneath them. Anna and Nuts looked at each other in alarm and got back on the ladder.

"Where are you going?" Anna asked. "We're trapped. Let's go down and turn ourselves in."

"Never surrender, Anna," Nuts said, climbing yet further up.

She hauled herself through the final hole and onto the very summit of the antenna. Among a mass of cables and Trixico broadcasting equipment, she came face-to-face with a pair of familiar eyes and a mop of scruffy brown hair.

"Norbert!" Nuts shouted, throwing her arms around him. He shrieked as her movement made the tower sway.

"What are you doing here? There are Hawks shooting at us," Norbert said, yanking her down below the railing.

"Yes, we know," Nuts said. She reached down to pull Anna onto the platform. "Someone didn't hide their bike. Long story."

Anna crawled into the corner and curled into a ball, then yanked her cravat off to use as a blindfold.

"Hi Anna," Norbert said.

"Just leave me alone," she snapped.

"Look," Norbert said, gently turning Nuts' head to face away from the city. "You can see the top of the wall."

The ring of concrete sliced through the cloud in an impossibly long arc. Beyond it, the outside world was covered with a sea of white cloud.

"The signal. It comes from outside. I'm sure of it," Norbert said.

Nuts stared at the wall in awe.

"I always thought it was like, this thick," she said, holding her hands shoulder-width apart. "But it's huge. You could drive a car around the top of that. Also, where are the lightning bolts coming off this thing, like on the poster?"

"I'll explain later. What now?" asked Norbert. "The Hawks are shooting at us. There's no way out."

"They were looking for you all morning. They went to Baz's house earlier and captured him. The Hawks discovered the television channel... and so did we when we went to Baz's house."

Norbert bared his teeth. He went pale as the gravity of the situation washed over him. It was entirely his fault that Baz had been captured, and now his only friend in the world was being shot at.

"So me and Anna... long story, but Anna's been reluctantly helping me. We..."

"Helping?" Anna yanked her blindfold up and sprang to her feet. She jabbed her index finger into Nuts' chest.

"You *kidnapped* me! You blackmailed me! I haven't been *helping*."

"Anyway," Nuts continued, swiping the accusatory finger away. "I wanted to find you, Norbert, to warn you that the Hawks were after you. We broke into Baz's house for clues, found the Beast Battle channel and then hid under the bed because more Hawks arrived. Then you will never guess who showed up."

"Okay," said Norbert, trying to process it. Another gunshot whistled past the antenna, missing the children. Norbert gasped. Anna cowered.

"Guess!" Nuts replied, excitedly.

"But you literally said I could never guess. Just tell me!"

A gunshot rang through the air.

"Trixie!" Anna interjected impatiently. "Can you two hurry up your chit-chat because we're being shot at. Let's just get our stories straight and head down."

Norbert crouched on the ground and put his ear to the cold metal. The faint clang of feet on a ladder vibrated through the tower.

"They're on their way up," he told the others.

Anna looked at the wave detector gun by Norbert's feet.

"Right, let's figure out our story. Sling that thing off the side and hope they don't see it," she said. "Then we can say Norbert wanted to see the view from up here. He didn't know it was illegal and didn't see the fifty signs warning not to do it. Me and Nuts were doing the right thing and coming to get him."

Nuts grabbed Anna's lapels and shook her.

"Anna, do the Hawks listen to reason? Do they listen to both sides of the argument and make a rational decision? Or...do they just make people disappear?"

"Disappearing is a myth," Anna said, her voice sounding less confident than usual.

"Are you willing to find out for sure?" Nuts asked.

The clang of feet on metal steps was now loud enough for all three of them to hear.

"What do you suggest, then? Shall we shoot them with Norbert's home-made egg poacher?" Anna said, her voice cracking as she blinked away tears.

Nuts wrenched the clothing from her backpack and stabbed her leg into the wingsuit her mum had made. Springing into a star shape, she raised her arms to reveal huge wings, double the size of the original. Norbert peeked over the edge and shuddered with fear, every hair on his body standing up on end.

"What on earth is that?" Anna asked. "You look like a bat."

"Exactly. We're going to fly out of here."

Nuts yanked a second skydiving suit from her pack.

"Norbert, you take my old one. Anna you hold me; this one has bigger wings."

"I'm not leaping off this tower," Anna said. "Are you insane? We'd fall to the floor like a sack of potatoes. I'm going to face the music."

Down through the ladder hole, Norbert made out the round, grey cap of a Hawk, clawing her way up the ladder in leather gloves. While Nuts did jumping jacks in her wingsuit, genuinely excited, Norbert reluctantly heaved his on, grimacing at the crude stitching on the arms. He looked out toward the wall.

"Go towards the wall, Nuts. I think we can get over it," Norbert said. "It's our only hope."

Nuts climbed onto the railing. "Anna, it'll be fine. I mean, I can't guarantee it. My mum's sewing can be a bit sketchy and by the looks of things, she used our old tent which rotted when I put away wet. But if the Hawks wanted to hear our side of the story, they wouldn't be shooting at us. Run, Anna! It's the only way."

Anna shook her head. Nuts shrugged.

The thump of boots against the metal ladder grew louder. "Norbert. Nutella. We know you are up there," came a bellowing voice from below.

Anna listened for her name, but it didn't come.

"They don't know I'm here," she said, her eyes wide with delight. She sprang across the platform and leaped onto Nuts' back.

"Go on then!" Anna said. "I need to disappear before they see me."

With Anna gripping around her shoulders like a backpack, Nuts spread out her wings. She leaned forward and pushed away from the tower, diving out into the sky. Norbert watched with one eye covered as Nuts fought the wind and steered out into a glide.

The crackling sound of electricity startled Norbert, and he turned to see a Hawk hauling herself onto the platform, stun stick in hand. Sweat dripped from her red face and she glared at him with venomous eyes.

"Norbert," she heaved. "You're coming with me."

In his mind, he was taken back to the toilet at Blackstone High, standing on the window sill. This time, there was no tree, only a mile high fall to earth. The panting Hawk crawled across the floor, swinging her stun stick at Norbert's ankles. He climbed onto the railing and leaned forward and launched himself out into the sky.

Chapter 30

"Another brilliant decision by Nuts."

The moment he left the platform, Norbert's stomach dropped. Despite holding his arms and legs out in a star jump, he fell like a stone, screaming. The ladders he had painstakingly hauled himself up passed by in seconds. Thwop. Thwop. Thwop. He spiralled down, fixated on the jagged fences below. His eyes streamed. His ears were deafened by the windblast.

Norbert craned his neck toward the wall and in the distance he saw Nuts and Anna, just a speck. As he focused on his friends, his fall stabilised and his body levelled out. Air filled the fabric and it took all his strength to keep his arms out straight and his legs apart. Like an opened parachute, the wind resistance slowed him, and the falling motion transformed to a horizontal glide. With enormous relief, he found himself blasting away from the metal antenna.

For a moment, his smile broke into a crack, and air blasted in, blowing out his cheeks like balloons. Tears streamed from his eyes. His muscles burned with the effort of holding his position against the hurricane wind. Throughout the blurry madness, he kept his gaze fixed on the wall.

As he hurtled closer to it, he realised he was too low to glide over the top. At the speed he was going, at least 100 miles per hour, he guessed, there would be nothing left of him but ketchup.

Norbert stretched out his fingers. He redoubled his effort to push his legs apart in the widest V the material would allow. He arched his back to get every bit of lift.

With seconds to go, the great white wall seemed to only grow taller. In the final few seconds he closed his eyes, unable to watch.

"Nooooorrbeeerrrrt!" came a shout.

He opened his eyes to see a splash of colour on a white backdrop. The afterlife, he thought? No. He was directly over the wall, gliding just metres above the gravel. Norbert kicked out his legs and ran in mid air as the surface rose up to meet him. SMACK.

In a tangle of arms and legs, he tumbled and somersaulted across the rugged surface of the wall. After a terrifying blur of sky and ground, he found himself sliding across gravel on all fours.

Suddenly, the ground gave way altogether and his legs dropped over the far side of the wall. In a split-second reaction, Norbert grabbed onto the sharp concrete lip and hung. His feet dangled. Below them, nothing but the decimated world beyond Puzzle Forest.

"Help!" he screamed, scrambling to toe the wall.

His pleas for help were met with the crunch of gravel. A hand reached over the edge and gripped his grazed forearm. Nuts hauled him up and onto the top of the wall, where Norbert flopped. Bruised and battered, but alive.

He sat up and picked gravel out of his knees.

"We made it," he croaked.

A little distance along the wall, Anna rocked on the lunar surface, knees to her chest.

"Why aren't they shooting?" Nuts asked.

Norbert looked back toward the antenna, which stuck out of the forest like a needle stabbed into moss.

"They won't be able to see us from there, even with binoculars," Norbert said. "Also, they probably assume we're dead. I expect they're looking around the base of the antenna for our bodies. Wouldn't you?"

Nuts nodded. "Absolutely. I gave us 50:50 at best."

Anna leaped to her feet.

"You said it would be fine! Why did you jump if you thought we might not make it?"

"What choice did we have? It was that or never get my A." Nuts' sentence tailed off and she looked at the floor.

"What?" Anna said.

"I needed my A for Antenna. I'm trying to get BASE. Building. Antenna. Span. Earth...which I already have."

"You are so, so dumb," Anna said, sitting back on the ground. "You have all these ideas, yet always choose the worst one."

"Good ideas are overrated," Nuts muttered.

"*All* of your ideas are overrated," Anna snapped back. "If you keep jumping off things wrapped up in a bed sheet, you're going to get your D for DEAD."

"Girls, please," Norbert said. "When they realise our bodies aren't at the base of the antenna, they might figure out we made it over here. We have to escape."

The three of them looked around for a way out. The wall stretched endlessly in both directions, its curve so slight that it almost looked straight.

Nuts grabbed Norbert by the shoulder. "Do you really believe there's life out there?" she asked.

"There's a television signal coming from the outside world. I'm sure of that," he said.

"Because of your toy gun?" Anna scoffed. "You'll die out there. The radiation will kill you in minutes, Norbert. There's no way out. Let's just wait for the Hawks, and tell the truth."

Nuts let out a yelp of frustration.

"No Anna! You still don't get it do you? Can you think of just one person in history who has gone in for questioning and come out again? Of course not. They take you in. You disappear. We're toast, Anna. But Norbert can leave. His wings are intact. There might be radiation or not, but at least he'll be choosing his destiny and not have it chosen for him."

"Freedom to choose death. Another brilliant decision by Nuts, the village idiot," Anna said.

Norbert stared at the world beyond Puzzle Forest. He began to wonder if his electronic device was reliable after all. Could it have picked up the wrong signal? Was he sure it came from outside of Puzzle Forest?

He thought of Baz, and the mess he had made. He thought of leaving

Nuts and Anna behind, and being captured by Hawks. What if Nuts was right, and they would be disappeared? How could he live with himself outside of Puzzle Forest, knowing that he brought that on their families?

"I can't leave. Not without you," he said.

Nuts punched him so hard on the shoulder that his bicep went numb. Anna was barely listening, and had spotted something in the distance.

"Look, over there. Is that a box, or something?"

After a few minutes of limping, the shape of a small building on top of the wall became more clear. They approached a concrete hut about the size of a garden shed, with glass windows on each of its four sides.

"It's a lookout tower," Norbert noted. "Let's go inside."

Chapter 31

"RUN."

Inside the hut was a folding metal chair and a spiral staircase which corkscrewed into the floor. On a window sill sat an empty mug, which Norbert found was stone cold. Next to it was a pair of binoculars, which he used to gaze out into the world beyond Puzzle Forest. He estimated that he could see one or or two miles, and it seemed devoid of human life. No roads or buildings, from what he could see, and the trees had no leaves.

"Found a great big arena with stupid battle robots?" Anna asked.

Norbert shook his head, and passed the binoculars to Nuts, who stuffed them into her backpack.

"Come on, we have to get moving," Nuts said. "If they have these guard towers all around the wall, it won't be long til they send up Hawks to look for us."

"I'll come with you," Anna said. "On the condition that when we get arrested you tell them that you kidnapped me."

"No deal," Nuts said. "If we get arrested I'm going to say you kidnapped me."

Anna gasped. Norbert shook his head and set off down the stairs. The two girls followed, scuffling to be first.

The spiral staircase curled deeper and deeper into the wall. Norbert was in a steady rhythm of padding down the steps, scraping his shoulder now and then on the rough stone wall, when the staircase stopped. All three of them piled up into a door.

Nuts cautiously opened it, finding a desolate corridor which curved away in both directions. It was wide enough to drive a car down and dimly lit by flickering fluorescent lights. The kids listened carefully, but could hear nothing except a background hum, which got louder when they put their ears to the cold, grey wall. It smelled musky and damp, like an underpass.

"Which way?" Norbert asked.

Anna had crudely tied together her own wrists with her cravat. Nuts noticed, and yanked it away before stuffing it in her backpack.

"Give it back!" Anna whispered.

She swiped at Nuts' bag but soon gave up.

"Shh!" Norbert said.

They crept along the hallway, led by Norbert, eventually reaching a metal door. Unlike the one that led to the guard tower, this had a square of glass at head height. They crouched below and listened. The hum was louder here. A whirring. And when Norbert listened more carefully, he could hear deep breathing. He began to rise up to peek through the glass.

Behind the door was a boxy, concrete cell, with a caged fluorescent light giving it a green tinge. Along one edge of the room was a raised block of concrete, with a dirty pillow and sheet. A metal toilet was in the corner, and in the centre of the room an exercise bike. On it was a woman, in orange shorts and a grimy white vest, pedalling furiously. She was stick thin except for her thighs and calves, which looked like they were carved out of oak. Her skin glistened with sweat, and her grey hair hung over her eyes.

Nuts and Anna joined Norbert at the window, and the three of them stared at the woman who was frantically pedalling towards nowhere. A green light glowed on the handlebars of the bike.

Suddenly she looked up and saw them at the window. Her feet slipped from the pedals, which span wildly and bashed her ankles. The woman's eyes were wide with horror and she wobbled and then pitched over backwards from the saddle, arms flailing. She scrambled to her feet and scurried to the window, wide, bloodshot eyes darting left and right. She mouthed some words but the trio couldn't hear through the thick glass. Norbert raised his eyebrows. Exasperated, the woman wrote in the glistening condensation on the glass window, tapping it madly.

NUR

"What does that even mean?" asked Nuts.

"It's backwards because she's writing from the inside" gulped Norbert. "She's telling us to RUN."

The pedals on the bike continued to whizz round, but the light on the handlebars was now orange. The woman looked more panicked than ever, and leaped back into the saddle, pedalling frantically to bring it back up to full speed. The light went green. She looked over through the glass once more and shook her head.

The lighting in the corridor changed from white to red and an alarm began to sound.

"Back to the roof. We'll never find our way out of here," said Anna.

The three of them raced back to the doorway from which they had emerged, and retraced their steps up the spiral staircase. Popping open the hatch, they emerged into the guard tower, hearts racing.

"What now?" said Nuts, gasping for breath.

"I'll go and see if there are ladders down the outside," yelled Norbert as he ran towards the outer edge.

"I'm not going outside the wall. It's death, Norbert. Deep down, you know that," shouted Anna.

Nuts smirked. "Whereas inside Puzzle Forest, we'll be welcomed back with open arms?"

Norbert reported back from the outside wall that he could see nothing along the edge, but had found a ladder in the distance that dropped back into Puzzle Forest.

"It's our only option," he said. "We just have to hope they're not waiting for us at the bottom of it."

Norbert followed Anna onto the top rung, and began the mile long descent into Puzzle Forest.

Chapter 32

"A gym?"

At the base of the ladder, Nuts tossed the last remnant of her wingsuit over the barbed wire fence. As Norbert dropped to the forest floor, he collapsed in pain, clutching his feet.

"That ladder was agony," he said.

"Get up," Anna said, brushing dirt from her school uniform. "We have to keep moving. Let's get into the forest before nightfall."

The forest around the city was vast, and even Nuts didn't know it all. She and Anna had spent their childhood in the woods of their home district, but over this side near the antenna, they had no idea where they were.

Nuts picked her way through wet bracken and slippery mud. The leafless canopy let through enough moonlight to see the ground in front of them, but not much more.

"Can we have a break?" asked Norbert.

The three of them slumped at the base of a tall oak tree, leaning on its jagged bark. Their breath misted in the winter air.

"What was that place?" asked Norbert, shuddering at the thought of the woman on the exercise bike.

"A gym?" Anna said.

Nuts laughed. A loud, fake laugh, repeating Anna's words.

"Shut up, Nuts! What do you think it is, then?" Anna said.

"A prison, obviously. I wonder how many people are in that place. I mean, you could never work it out. I doubt even they know," said Nuts.

Norbert squinted. "Well, they must have had architectural plans so I expect they do know, Nuts. And they must allocate cells to inmates, so they've got a database somewhere, probably on a computer. The fact the alarm system went off probably means it has sensors, so it must be somewhat sophisticated."

"Oh blah, blah, blah," Anna said.

"Shhh," Nuts said. "How many people are in there?"

"We know it's a mile high," Norbert said. "Say, three or four hundred floors."

Nuts and Anna shrugged approvingly.

"Let's guess Puzzle Forest is 25 miles wide, and the circumference of a circle is pi."

"What are you even talking about?" Nuts said. "We want to know how many people are in it. Not how many pies."

"At a guess, half a million prison cells," Norbert said, swallowing as he processed the vast number.

"Is that where all the people who disappear go?" Nuts asked.

Anna shuddered at the thought.

"We don't *know* it's not a gym," she muttered.

"So what now?" asked Nuts. "We can't go back to the city. We're wanted, and if we get captured we could end up on a treadmill for the rest of our lives. Let's build a camp and figure out a plan in the morning."

Anna walked away from the tree and began gathering sticks for her own den.

"I'm going home tomorrow," she said resolutely. "I'm going to explain to my parents that I was kidnapped. And they'll make the necessary arrangements with the city."

"Anna, are you crazy?" Nuts demanded. "We watched Trixie kill two Hawks. I bet they have figured that out by now, and they won't risk that information getting out."

"I didn't *watch* anything. I might have heard a mug fall from a table, or something," Anna said.

"Two mugs, wasn't it?" Norbert joked under his breath.

"And anyway," Anna continued. "I'm not foraging for mushrooms with you for the rest of my life. I'll take my chances with the Hawks. My mother will take care of everything."

"For us, too?" Norbert asked.

"Good night. Don't wake me in the morning. I need my eight hours."

Norbert woke up with mud on his cheek and soaking wet clothes. He and Nuts had leaned a few sticks into an A-frame, but snow had fallen through the gaps and blanketed him.

Anna had already risen and was putting the sticks from her den back where she had found them. Norbert wondered if there was anyone else in the world who would go to the effort of tidying up a forest. She straightened her school uniform and brushed the mud from her shoes with a pine frond.

"All dressed up with nowhere to go?" Nuts yawned.

"Mother says that you can tell a person's value the moment you set eyes on them."

"Your mum is so judgy," Nuts said.

"She is not judgy at all. Anyway, at least she doesn't wear slippers to work."

"My mum did that ONCE."

"Please, can you two stop arguing? At least you've got mums," Norbert said.

He sighed, and set about picking up the sticks Anna had returned, for his own den. While Nuts remained on her bed of moss, Norbert reinforced the roof of their shelter.

"I assume we're staying here another night," he said, sadly.

"I'm not. I'm going home now. I'm going to explain everything to my parents. We haven't done anything so bad that we'd go to prison. We climbed the antenna. So what? And we BASE jumped onto the wall. We had a quick peek inside before going down the ladder. Is that so bad?"

She waited a moment for a reaction.

"Okay, okay," Nuts said, picking leaves from her hair. "Anna, wait for us!"

The three of them trekked into the forest with the wall looming behind them. Eventually they made it to the periphery, a road which encircled the entire city. It was empty, since few residents of Puzzle Forest had any reason to come out this far.

Nuts and Anna peered through the trees towards the houses in the distance.

"Do you recognise any street names?" Nuts asked.

"I think this must be district four. We need to go clockwise," she said.

The day passed deep in the forbidden woods, picking their way through trails and staying hydrated by eating mouthfuls of crunchy snow. Every now and then, they were high enough to see the wall in the distance, and it made Norbert feel sick.

Anna marched ahead, eager to distance herself from her supposed 'kidnappers'. Nuts and Norbert followed, not sure what they would do when Anna made it to her parents' home.

"Are you okay?" Nuts asked Norbert as the afternoon drew on. "You've barely said a word all day."

Norbert trudged on in silence as he shaped the thoughts in his mind to answer.

"Not really, he said. "I just feel lost. Every time I have someone to hold on to....every time I have a place to belong...it disappears. My parents. Gone. But I got by with Owly. Gone. Even Baz. Gone. I must be cursed or something."

"You have me," Nuts said, punching Norbert gently on the shoulder. He smiled.

"What next?" he said. "I keep searching and searching for stability, and it keeps getting further away. It feels like drowning."

As the morning drew on, the trio reached familiar territory, with Nuts' tower block looming in the distance. Anna set off across the park that led to her suburb, sticking close to the bushes. Nuts and Norbert followed.

"Stop following me!" she said. "You're not coming to my house. Twice you've been to my house. First time you burgled it. Second time you ruined my life. So don't expect a third invite."

"So, that's it?" Nuts said. "You're just going to go home, claim we kidnapped you, and pretend you saw nothing inside the wall? Baz's flat - I suppose you were never there?"

"Yes. I didn't see anything. So basically that means we were never there,"

Anna said.

"Could you really go on, knowing you're surrounded by a five hundred storey prison? It's lies upon lies, and anyone who questions it gets slung into jail."

Nuts was furious now. Anna just shook her head as if to cleanse it of the truth.

"Puzzle Forest is the last refuge on Earth, Nuts. Bad people have to be put in jail for their crimes. I don't know how they decide on it, I'm just a kid. Maybe they like to do exercise. But all I know is that I was happy here until a few days ago, and I can be happy here again. Don't you miss your mum? Just because *he* doesn't have a family, doesn't mean we have to lose ours."

Anna pointed at Norbert, and her cold words made the hairs stand up on his neck. He thought of his parents getting into the taxi and leaving for the airport. For years he had lived in hope that they would walk back through the front door. It was bleak, but he had a roof over his head and food on the table. Now he had even lost that.

Norbert scrubbed a hand over his eyes.

"She's right, Nuts. Go home. This is all my fault, and I've done enough damage."

With that, Norbert set off into the bushes, heading back into the forest.

Nuts shook her head. "Anna, you've got a badge where your heart should be," she said.

Anna marched into her suburb, while Nuts hurried to catch up with Norbert.

Chapter 33

"Anna White is wanted."

For the first time in days, the sun shone across the city. Anna smiled when she saw her familiar street sign, and stooped to wipe the snow from it. The neighbourhoods in Puzzle Forest were almost identical, and yet some were still considered better than others. In Anna's street, the home owners had a strict set of rules to keep their lawns mowed and fences painted. It was peak Puzzle Forest, and was regularly used in photo shoots for the official city newspaper.

As she passed her neighbours' homes, Anna noticed a sign stuck into her front garden. On it was a face. Her own face. It was the same picture her mother had chosen for her campaign for class president. Anna couldn't quite read the text, and assumed it said MISSING. She smiled, straightened her cravat and...wait. She swallowed, her face pale. Peering closer, she read the sign.

Anna White, WANTED for Crimes against the City. Dangerous, do not approach. Call HAWKS on 111.

Dangerous? Crimes? She hid against the trunk of a tree and reread the sign several times. Distracted by a knocking noise, Anna looked around to identify its source. Up and down the street, every single house had her face staring back at her. In the distance she saw someone hammer a sign into a well shovelled lawn. She couldn't believe what she was seeing. Her own mother.

Anna's legs buckled and she crouched in the shadow of the oak. It still bore the marks of a swing which her mother had rallied the neighbourhood committee to remove. Anna wiped away tears with her cravat. She looked at the badges - campaigner, spy, timekeeper - and hurled it into the snow.

"Anna, is that you?" came a voice from across the street.

A woman who had babysat her as a child stood on her lawn, snow shovel in hand.

"Hi Karen, it's a big misunderstanding," Anna said, with a sickly smile. "None of this is true."

Karen ran into her house and reemerged with a phone at her ear, its cord stretched to breaking point.

"Stay right where you are, you criminal!" she shouted.

Anna took off, tearing down the street towards the forest.

Chapter 34

"You're a bad girl and you need to be arrested."

"Oh Nuts. My beautiful girl. What are you doing here?" Kara shouted, bringing her daughter in for a hug.

"I'm so angry with you for breaking the law!" she continued, pushing her away. "I'm calling the Hawks immediately. Step aside!"

Nuts was confused by the sudden change of heart. "Mum, it's okay. I didn't do anything wrong."

"Get out of the way!" Kara called again. Nuts edged against the hallway wall, but it seemed pointless because she wasn't in her mum's way.

"I must get to the phone immediately and call the Hawks," Kara shouted. She looked Nuts in the eyes and kicked a rucksack, which toppled through the lounge doorway.

"What the..." Nuts began, but Kara slapped a hand onto her daughter's mouth and pushed her towards the front door.

"You're a bad girl and you need to be arrested. Stay here in this room. You are not to leave this house until the Hawks arrive."

Kara ran to the phone and picked up the receiver. Nuts looked at the backpack, then at her mum.

"Are you for real? You're calling the Hawks on me?"

"Of course I am! You need to be stopped. Now stay right where you are! One. One...."

Kara looked her daughter in the eyes as she defiantly tapped it a third time.

"No, don't do it Mum. Let me explain," Nuts pleaded, stepping towards the kitchen.

"There's nothing to explain. You've broken the law."

Nuts heard the line connect, bringing with it the muffled voice of a Hawk.

"Come quickly, Nuts has returned home and I've captured her," Kara said.

Nuts mouthed the word 'No!' She backed up towards the front door, brushing against a *'Live. Laugh. Love Trixie'* sign.

Kara spoke into the phone. "Yes, she is still here but she's trying to escape. She's got a brown backpack."

Nuts shook her head in disbelief. She opened the front door, crushed by her mother's betrayal.

"BACKPACK," Kara shouted into the phone.

Nuts was completely confused, but saw her mum eyeing a fat leather bag in the doorway of the lounge. She grabbed it and left the flat.

"I've got to go," Kara said. "She's trying to escape."

She hung up the phone and, in a slow motion dawdle, followed Nuts out of the front door. In a flash of copper hair, Nuts jumped onto her bike and pedalled along the gangway.

Cars screeched to a halt at the foot of the tower block. Kara cried loudly at her front door, shaking her fist.

"You won't get away with this Nuts! Turn yourself in!"

Her neighbours poked their heads out of their doors and saw the girl racing along the gallery towards the lift. The elevator opened and two Hawks stood with stun guns at the ready.

"Freeze!" they shouted. "You are wanted!"

Nuts skidded into the stairwell and bombed down the stairs. The Hawks chased after her but their boots were no match for her bicycle.

She burst out into the world at the base of her tower block, to see yet another Hawk vehicle arrive. A car chased her into the park, tearing up the grass and blasting through sand pits. Nuts zig-zagged past the swing set but found herself cornered.

"Stop! You are under arrest!" the Hawk said.

Nuts had no choice but to smash through a hedge and hope for the best. She tucked her head down and closed her eyes as she hit the spiky tangle of branches. Nuts was catapulted over the handlebars and landed heavily at the edge of the periphery road. Dazzled by the lights of yet more Hawk cars, she scrambled across the street without her bike and slipped into the woods. There, she ran and ran, jumping over streams and ducking under branches, until her heart pounded and the sound of sirens finally disappeared.

Chapter 35

"Those aren't pyjamas."

Norbert had watched the drama unfold from high in a tree. He had seen Nuts disappear into her block and wished he could warn her as Hawk after Hawk arrived in the car park below. By the time Nuts had escaped on her bike, Norbert had climbed down and hidden deeper into the woods, to ensure he wasn't captured too.

Norbert climbed a tall beech tree that evening, which he estimated was a mile from the point where Nuts had re-entered the forest. Earlier on he had seen the distant glimpse of torch light, which he assumed were Hawks searching the dense undergrowth for the runaways.

It had been hours since the last of the Hawks had moved on, and Norbert wished he had arranged a meeting point with Nuts. It was too risky to go back to Kara's flat, or even the spot where Nuts had smashed through the hedge and abandoned her bike. The Hawks would doubtless be waiting there.

He recalled the den where Nuts used to all meet up with her friends, but figured the Hawks would have found that. Norbert could attempt to retrace his steps to where they slept last night, but wasn't sure he could find the way.

He sat on a thick bough, leaning back against the rough bark of the tree. It was time to head down and build a shelter, but having not eaten for days, the prospect of foraging in the snow felt impossible. As he looked at the ground below, he smiled, imagining how Nuts would probably just jump and hope for the best. With that thought, he remembered the lake where they had first tested the wingsuit. Perhaps Nuts would have the same thought and return there?

Norbert carefully climbed down the branches of the tree to the forest floor. He set off through the dark night to a spot dangerously close to Nuts' home district, because only there could he pick up the trail to the lake.

A journey which would have flown on the back of Nuts' bike took hours, and by the end of it Norbert was plodding at a glacial pace, picking frozen berries to give him the energy to continue.

The darkness of the trees opened up to the lake, shimmering blue and silver in the moonlight. Norbert scanned the shoreline but could see nothing, and felt a crushing sense of defeat. But as he looked down at the sand, he spotted footprints. Since he was wearing Nuts' spare shoes, he was able to tell they were a perfect fit.

Her tracks stopped at the base of the enormous tree from which she had jumped, weeks ago. Norbert climbed from limb to limb, and finally he saw her shoe, laces characteristically undone, hanging down from a high branch. With renewed energy, Norbert climbed up and bashed her foot.

Nuts awoke with a start and recoiled, slipping from her nook and grabbing on as she fell. Her legs gripped around the branch and she swung upside down, staring at Norbert as he came into focus in the moonlight.

"You found me!" she said, much too loudly. "It is so good to see you!"

The two of them sat side by side, staring out over the lake which sparkled in the moonlight. Nuts recounted the story of her mum and showed Norbert the backpack.

"It was like she was under a spell," Nuts said. "Never thought my own mum would call the Hawks on me, but I watched her do it. She dialled the number, spoke to them right in front of me and wanted to trap me and turn me in. But even more odd than that, was the backpack. I couldn't understand why she told the Hawks I had a backpack, when I didn't. I lost my backpack with the stun gun ages ago. There was one on the floor though, so I grabbed it. It was like she was telling me not to get out, but didn't really stop me. She was telling me I had a backpack when I didn't. Maybe she's gone a bit mad."

"What's in the backpack?" Norbert asked.

"I dunno, it's locked," she said, retrieving a heavy brown leather bag, hooked over a branch. She thumbed the four dials on a metal padlock.

"It's a combination lock, and I've tried everything I can think of. My birth year, our house number twice. I mean, that is everything I can think of. I don't want to just rip it open because it'll be so annoying having to carry around a bag that won't close. Then I tried to do that anyway but I'm not strong enough. If we have to, I could probably gnaw through it with my teeth."

Norbert studied the lock and felt the heavy bag.

"It smells of food," he said. "It sounds to me like your mum was being watched, and knew it. Maybe Hawks with binoculars were looking through the windows, or perhaps microphones or videocameras have been set up in your flat. She wanted to make sure those Hawks saw her doing the right thing; capturing you. Otherwise she'd end up in the wall, right? That's why she had to phone it in and tell you not to leave."

"Right!" said Nuts, excitedly. "But she didn't want me to get captured, so she made sure I got out of there."

"Yes, that's what I think." Norbert nodded.

"But if she wanted me to have this backpack, which feels like it has some clothes in it, why would she lock it?" Nuts wondered.

Norbert looked at the thick leather flap and the metal D-shaped ring locked shut.

"Perhaps because she had this bag sat in the lounge, ready for you, and knew that at any point the Hawks could come and raid her flat for clues. She wanted to make sure it was locked so she could say 'I have no idea what Nuts has packed in that bag, I can't open it'. The lock gives her an excuse to play dumb."

Nuts sniffed the bag for clues as to its contents, and shook it by her ear.

"How about we try every possible code, starting at 0001 and working our way up to 9999," Nuts suggested. "How long would that take?"

"Well, let's say it takes 5 seconds per number, then that's fifty thousand seconds, which would take about....800 minutes....so.....13 hours. Shall we do that, in shifts? Say, two hours each, while the other one sleeps?"

"Yes!" said Nuts. "Good night."

"Wait, I can't sleep up in the branches. I might fall. Let's go and build a shelter by the lake."

At the foot of the trees, they cobbled together a basic shelter from leaves and branches. Norbert rolled the digits around to 0-0-0-0 and braced himself for the long night ahead. As the fourth zero clunked into place, the lock snapped open. His eyes opened wide and he tapped Nuts wildly.

"Nuts, it was zero zero zero zero, ha ha!"

They both laughed, and Norbert unthreaded the lock and opened the leather flap. Nuts reached into the bag and grabbed the first item, which was a sandwich wrapped up in string. Beneath it were several more, a few apples and pasties. It had been days since the duo had eaten anything more than berries, and they eagerly ate the picnic.

Beneath the food was some clothing.

"My mum is obsessed with me being too cold," Nuts smiled. "And you too, by the looks of things. She's packed loads."

Norbert thought of his own mum, pulling his hood over his hair and kissing him on the forehead before school. He pictured his lounge, and the vast blue maps of the Asantic Ocean which now covered its walls. Was Owly there, waiting for him to come home from school, as he had waited so long for his parents to come home from holiday? It was too much for even Norbert to process.

"What do you think happened to Anna?" Norbert asked.

Nuts shook her head.

"Honestly, I bet she threw us under the bus and said it was all my fault. She's probably in bed right now, head on a soft pillow, really pleased with herself."

"Mum made me some pink pyjamas. That's cute," she said, sniffling.

Norbert reached for the cuff and lifted it, revealing a piece of material connecting the arm and the body.

"Those aren't pyjamas, Nuts. She's made you a new wingsuit."

Anna stared up through the roof of her den. The moon hung in the night sky and she focused with all her might on the patches of dark and light rock on its surface. In a world turned upside down, she found a sense of solace in seeing one thing that had stayed the same. It was the same moon, she thought, that she and her mother had stared at from the kitchen window. She would be wearing her spare school uniform for indoors, waiting for her dear mum to take a tray of cookies out of the oven. She reached across her chest slowly and placed her hand on her own shoulder, imagining how it would feel to have the warmth of her mother's touch.

Her peaceful thoughts were interrupted by the memory of her mum hammering in those wanted posters. How could she possibly believe that her own daughter deserved prison, just for climbing the antenna? What must the news be saying about her to make her own family disown her in total shame?

Anna shut her eyes, hoping that tomorrow she could find the strength to face another day. A day of foraging in the undergrowth for acorns and berries like a wild animal. And to what end, she thought? A lifetime alone, running scared in the cold, dark woods did not sound much better than being trapped in that wall with a cycling machine and bowl of gruel.

Anna sobbed until there were no tears left to cry, and fell asleep with her head on a pillow of damp moss.

The decision of what to do with the rest of her life, it turned out, was made for her. In the darkest part of the night, a pair of strong hands grabbed her, and a third muffled her scream as she awoke.

"Anna, you're coming with us," they said as they bundled her wriggling, screaming body into a thick brown sack.

Chapter 36

"I've got nothing to lose."

Norbert watched the sun rise over the shimmering lake. It was impossible to sleep, anyway, with the cold and Nuts' snoring. Up high in the tree, life felt simple and for a moment, and if he really concentrated, he could focus on the calm water and the rustling of leaves. Within seconds, though, the reality of his predicament came flooding back.

He thought of Owly and wished for nothing more than to talk to him. Was he even real? He could picture his house so clearly. The greenhouse in the garden. The apple his mum had left on the worktop when she left for holiday. But it all seemed impossible.

He tried to recall what he had read about parallel universes, and whether he could somehow have slipped from one world to another. Or was he dreaming? Was he actually in a hospital following his bicycle crash, and was Puzzle Forest a figment of his imagination. He pinched the skin on his forearm until it hurt.

Nuts pulled herself up to his branch, shaking him from his thoughts.

"Are you alright, Norbert?" she asked.

He shook his head.

"I want to go home. I know where I am, in Puzzle Forest by the lake. But I feel totally lost, and it makes me feel like I'm going mad, or imagined my home. You think I'm making it up when I say I have a robot owl friend, don't you?"

Nuts shook her head.

"When you first told me, of course I thought it was impossible. Bits of electronics can talk. I get that. The radio, telephone, television can all talk, but they can't *think*."

"Owly could think," Norbert said. "I swear, Nuts. Not at first, but I spent four years programming him and he could think. He could make up jokes and empathise and worry. He could love, I think, although he never would have admitted it."

"I thought you were mad when you first said that," Nuts said. "But when I was in Baz's flat and saw those robot beast things on his television, I immediately thought about your owl. It made me realise you probably didn't make it up."

"It's hard to imagine things you haven't seen," he said.

"So what are we going to do?" Nuts asked, legs swinging in the cold morning breeze.

The word 'we' complicated things further. Norbert had many months fending for himself, for what good it had done him.

"I don't think my home is in Puzzle Forest, Nuts," Norbert said sadly. He stared down towards the undergrowth several storeys below. "I am sure my house didn't look like Anna's or yours. I would have recognised one of the streets, or neighbourhoods, surely? And I know about things you wouldn't have been taught in school."

Nuts threw a twig down to the ground.

"So, you think there's life outside Puzzle Forest? It didn't look like there was, when we were up on that wall. No buildings, in the distance. Was there?"

"No. But there's nothing for me inside these walls," Norbert said. "I can't stay on the run forever."

"Are we willing to risk death to find out?" Nuts asked.

"Look at this." Norbert reached over and picked up Nuts' backpack. On it was a clasp which had held the padlock in place.

"Look at this metal ring."

Nuts felt its smooth surface and poked her fingertip through the hole.

"What about it?" she asked.

"Do you know anyone who works in a foundry?"

"What's a foundry?" Nuts replied.

"Exactly. You don't know what it is, and that's because almost everyone here does paperwork, right? Everyone seems to be in the business of writing reports and filing them. So who made this buckle?"

Nuts examined the D-shaped loop, and its perfectly formed base plate where it connected to the leather bag.

"It's not hand made. It's too perfect, so it must be liquid steel poured into a mould," Norbert said. "And that's fine - perhaps somewhere in this vast city is a foundry, tucked away. But then where do they get the raw iron from? Is there a mine? A smelter to crush up huge rocks and heat them up to extract iron ore? Surely not."

"Right, so where did this buckle come from?" Nuts asked.

"If I had to guess, it comes from outside that wall. Think of your flat. Your shoes, the telephone, the carpet. So much stuff. Can it really all be made inside the walls? There are loads of factories, but I don't think there are enough to make all the different items we see. Dials for ovens. Screws. Concrete. It's not possible."

Nuts flicked a leaf down into the abyss beneath them.

"So, you're going to leave me here and go?" she said. "That's what my dad did. And all that's left of him is a photo my mum has, of his running shoes and a pile of...well...nothing. It's hard to look at."

"I have to, Nuts. I don't have a mum at home making me a backpack of sandwiches. I've got nothing to lose," Norbert said.

Nuts stood up on the branch, threw her backpack on and hopped down the branches. "Well that's that decided then. Thanks a lot, FRIEND."

Norbert followed after Nuts, who grumpily whacked through the undergrowth with a stick.

"Wait!" he called.

Nuts relented and the two faced each other in a clearing.

"I would love you to come with me, Nuts. But I can't put that on you. I've made enough of a mess already. Baz has vanished. I've lost my parents. My home. Owly. I'm like toxic sludge. Everyone who gets close to me disappears, and you're too important."

Their discussion was interrupted by the crunch of twigs. Norbert darted to the trunk of a tree and stood with his back to it, pulling Nuts beside him. The two stood in terrified silence and listened for the source of the sound. It had been too loud to be an animal or falling acorn.

Then it happened again, this time from the direction of the lake. The two of them looked at each other, their eyes wide with fear. Nuts cocked her head to one side and pointed in the direction they should run. Norbert nodded.

Nuts darted into the undergrowth with Norbert following close behind. They crashed through the bushes, scrambling through wet mud and weaving a path between trees. Norbert tripped on a fallen branch and fell face first into the snow. Nuts skidded to a halt, looking back to rescue her friend. At that moment Norbert saw a dark shape emerge from the undergrowth and a sack was slammed over Nuts' head and shoulders. She wriggled violently and kicked at the thick material, but it was too late. Before he could even shout, the same thing happened to him, and he was encased up to his feet.

"Let me out!" shouted Nuts, kicking against the inside of the bag.

Norbert could hear his friend, but thought shouting was futile. He instead focused on a tiny gap in the neck of the sack through which he could see the flash of leaves as they swung their way through forest trails.

He felt sick with anger and sadness, that a future inside that prison awaited him. He thought of that desperate woman who had mouthed the word 'run'. If only he had taken the advice and leapt from the wall when he had the chance.

Nuts, meanwhile, grumbled and punched at the brown matting of the sack. The journey dragged on endlessly, and every time Nuts shouted "Where are you taking us?", Norbert heard a sickening thump.

He knew that the forest around the city was six or seven miles deep, so they would soon reenter a world of concrete. Any minute now, he thought, we will be bundled into the boot of a Hawk car.

After what must have been hours, the two sacks were dumped onto the floor, and it felt soft like grass. A voice spoke, for the first time since they had been captured.

"If you make a noise, we'll shoot you. Kick at the sack if you understand."

Both sacks twitched as the frightened legs kicked outwards. The gruff, male voice continued.

"I'm going to let you out now, and we're going to have a talk. Keep your mouths shut."

Norbert kicked at his sack, and Nuts heard him do so and copied. The ropes holding the sacks were opened and the captives crawled out onto the floor. He had expected to come out of this ordeal in a prison cell or a police station. In fact, they were on the forest floor, surrounded by trees that stretched as far as he could see in every direction. As his eyes adjusted to the light, he saw black boots with a Hawk insignia branded into the heel.

Chapter 37

"So where are we?"

N orbert looked around at the trees, massaging his neck to bring it back to life. He felt the criss-cross indentation of the sack cloth on his cheeks. The man in boots angrily snapped his fingers to get his and Nuts' attention. He paced around the two kids, a stun gun swinging from his belt. His hair was matted with dirt and died pinky-red. His lip bore the mark of a piercing, now partly healed.

"We know who you are. Well, we know who *you* are," he said, pointing at Nuts. "Do you know who we are?"

Nuts spat on the floor. "Does that answer your question?" she said.

The Hawk looked down at the globule and laughed. "Yes, it does answer my question. You think I'm a Hawk, right? The boots. The stun stick. Yeah, I'll give you that. Guys, come and say hello."

Norbert and Nuts heard rustling in the surrounding bushes and a ring of people emerged. First a woman about the same age as Kara. Then a teenager, eyes covered by a mask. They kept coming out until at least ten of them were standing in a wide circle in the forest clearing. They wore tattered jeans and jumpers patched at the elbows. Some of them covered their faces with bandanas.

Norbert and Nuts huddled even closer together, back-to-back on the leaf litter.

"I'm not a Hawk. Not for a long time, anyway. I'm Stew. We're Rebels. We live out here in the forest, free from the slavery in Puzzle Forest. Please, take a seat, everyone."

The onlookers rolled a few fallen logs into the clearing and perched on the cold, wet bark.

"We have heard stories about you for a few weeks now," Stew said. "We know you climbed the antenna, and we saw the posters. We knew you'd come out to the woods eventually, so we tracked you. I'm sorry we had to put you into sacks. We value our secrecy above all else. That's how we survive out here. You don't know this, but you were only a few hours from being captured down by the Hawks. They were *this* close, and we had to move fast and get you out of there."

Nuts was first to ask questions, as Norbert was still frozen like a deer in the headlights.

"How do we know you don't work for Trixie?" she said, summoning every bit of courage.

"Because if we worked for Trixie, we'd have killed you already," Stew said, with a sigh.

"So where are we?" Nuts asked.

"That's not something I can share. Like I say, the only thing keeping us alive out here is the fact the Hawks can't find us. If you know our location, there's a risk that one day you'll be captured and they'll make you talk. They have terrible, terrifying ways of making people tell their secrets."

Norbert cleared his throat.

"I have a question, if that's okay? I'm Norbert, by the way. This is Nuts." The group fell silent, curious to hear from the young boy. "Why did you risk coming out of your hiding place to rescue us?"

"Good question, Norbert. And don't worry, I'm one of the good guys now. Try to be, anyway." The group chuckled and Stew continued. "We tapped into the Hawks' radio channel and we heard them chase you up the antenna. Then you just...disappeared. But not in the usual way. You came back. Then we saw all the wanted posters going up around the place, and the increase in Hawk patrols in your neighbourhood. The higher ups, they're obsessed with finding you. Why? We need to know what happened up there on that antenna."

Nuts and Norbert looked at each other and nodded. They felt a relief that they had company, but at the same time, a mounting weight of worry as it became apparent they were no ordinary fugitives.

"Before we get into that," Stew said. "Let's get inside."

He nodded to a dirty-faced young girl with dreadlocked blond hair. She saluted her boss and scratched around in the dirt, uncovering a wooden hatch. A set of stairs descended into the ground and the group began to file down. The forest clearing gradually emptied, and Stew motioned to Nuts and Norbert to descend into the depths.

"How do we know these guys are not about to take us straight to jail? Sell us for the reward," Nuts whispered.

Norbert looked back and reached out his hand.

"Maybe they are, maybe they aren't. But what choice do we have? Run, out into the forest? Sleep another night in a tree, and another, and another? When does it end, Nuts? Come on, let's see where this goes."

The two kids stepped down into the darkness, and the hatch was closed above their heads.

Chapter 38

"You little gnarler."

Norbert stepped carefully down the thick wooden boards, buried into golden earth at each end. The subterranean world was dimly lit by candles and torches, tucked into enclaves scooped out of the earthen walls. The damp air felt heavy in his lungs, like the interior of a garden shed that sat closed all winter.

The steps ended with a straight tunnel, and Norbert couldn't help but think of the prison they had entered just yesterday. Where the geometric staircase drilled into the Wall felt robotic, this haphazard burrow felt like the work of an animal. The tunnel weaved through the earth, up and down, left and right, with wooden beams fighting back against the bulging world above. Stew and his entourage led the way, ducking under overhead cables. Finally they reached a pair of ornately carved doors, which looked otherworldly and out of place in this chaotic den.

The rabble became silent and Stew knocked on the door.

"Come," said a female voice. Stew held it open for Norbert and Nuts, and ushered the rest of his entourage back to their stations.

Nuts and Norbert entered a large and luxurious chamber, with ornate rugs on the floor and paintings hung on whitewashed walls. A few doorways led off to the sides, and in the back of the room a few steps led up to a platform, on which was a throne, its gold paint flaking.

A woman with skin as white as paper and thin black lips looked down at them. She wore a tatty, ruffled blouse that made Norbert think of a school teacher from a bygone era. She looked down on Nuts and Norbert with a look of mild disappointment, which reminded him that he hadn't showered for days.

"This is Lily, our leader," said Stew.

"So, you're the troublemakers we've been hearing so much about." Her voice was lethargic, as if the sentence was one long sigh.

"We're not troublemakers," said Nuts, irritably. "We did nothing wrong."

Lily chuckled. "Oh, don't worry. We're all troublemakers who have done nothing wrong, down here, so you'll fit right in. Do you want to hear what I have to say, or did you come here to moan?"

"Whatever," Nuts muttered.

"I'm Lily, and I am the leader of the Rebels. We have two goals. Firstly, to provide a safe place for those fleeing the regime. Secondly, we seek to overthrow Trixie and free Puzzle Forest."

Nuts gasped. A natural rebel who had spoken out of turn for her entire life, even she was shocked by the statement. Lily smirked.

"It's okay, we can speak freely here. The only place on Earth where you can, so you might as well enjoy it. You look hungry. Would you like to eat?"

The kids nodded.

"Stewart, please give these two a chamber to clean up in and come to my dining room in one hour. You should join us for dinner too, and also will you check if the scouts were successful in their mission?"

Stew nodded and backed out of the room, escorting Norbert and Nuts through a labyrinth of hallways which got narrower and narrower, until he opened a wooden door.

"Here is your room. It's not exactly a house, but a lot more comfortable than the branch you've been sleeping on. Here, you'll need these."

Stew handed Norbert a box of matches, to be used to light stoves and candles throughout the underground den. Norbert gratefully entered the room. It was sparsely furnished with two bunk beds, cobbled together from wood of every shape and colour. They thanked Stew, who said he would come and collect them in half an hour for dinner.

Nuts dumped her backpack onto the floor and leaped up to the top bunk in one go. Norbert took the one below her, and lit a candle next to the bed so they could see better. They exhaled, trying to make sense of what had happened.

"Do you regret meeting me, Nuts?" Norbert asked. "One day you were living a good life, watching Billy the Carrot and playing in the woods. Now you're hiding out in an underground bunker."

Nuts hung her head over the bunk, a leaf falling from her hair.

"Norbert, not long ago Mum came home all excited. She dragged me into the bathroom because she was convinced that the television was listening to us. Was it, by the way?"

"Probably," Norbert said. "Go on."

"So she's super excited. 'Guess what I've got!' and all that. You know what it was?"

Norbert shook his head.

"Two eggs."

"Okay..." Norbert was confused by this. Nuts, whose face was going red from being upside down, continued.

"So we had to walk to a guy's flat on the 13th floor and pick up the eggs, which were illegal of course. Don't ask me where he got hold of them. Mum planned this elaborate story about why we were walking to his house in case the Hawks stopped us. Mum even changed her mind at one point and said 'No, it's too reckless Nuts. What am I doing?' Anyway we got the eggs and she made some pastry thing, which incidentally you ate when you first arrived."

"Got it. So, I asked you if you regretted meeting me. You replied that your mum bought some eggs," summarised Norbert.

Nuts returned to her bed and tried to reach the ceiling with her feet, scratching the mud with her toes, which sprinkled into her eyes.

"Puzzle Forest is so mind-numbingly bland, Norbert, that eggs count as adventure. Every day we go to the same school and sing the same songs, eat the same food on the same tray and recite the same nonsense. Walking home with a couple of eggs in my pocket counts as wild excitement."

She swung back down, hair flicking across Norbert's face, blue eyes wide.

"Then you arrived, you little gnarler," she smiled. "And since then everything has gone bananas. One minute I'm jumping off an antenna. Next, we discovered the wall is a giant prison. I've been chased by Hawks multiple times, and now we're in an underground Rebel base."

Norbert nodded.

"I'm scared out of my mind. I love it! I can never, ever go back to sneaking around with a stolen egg. I want to fight the system, destroy everything!"

The idea of anarchy was horrifying for Norbert, but he understood the strange logic to it. "But remember that woman on the bike. That wall is terrifying, and it isn't short of room for two more inmates."

Nuts shrugged.

"The whole place is a prison. What does it matter whether you're forced to pedal a bicycle or sing Trixie songs?"

Their conversation was interrupted by a knock at the door.

"It's time for dinner," Stew said. "With Lily."

Nuts jumped down from her top bunk and rubbed her hands together.

"Remember, she runs this place," Stew said. "So, don't forget to, you know, be polite. You won't get many opportunities to dine with the top brass."

"Yeah, yeah," Nuts said. She licked her fingers and used them to smear her hair away from her forehead. "I'm highly educated. What's on the menu? Has she got eggs?"

Stew gave a slightly worried smile, then led the way to Lily's dining room.

Chapter 39

"We don't believe that rubbish here."

“This is the best den I have ever seen, and I've made a lot of them” Nuts said.

“Hmm” Lily said, motioning for the kids to sit. “It's a little more than a ‘den’. We house hundreds of people in a network of tunnels several miles long. But thank you, nonetheless.”

The walls, carved from bedrock, curved up to a ceiling with a chandelier. Classical music played quietly from an old battery powered tape recorder. The wooden table in the centre of the room could have sat twelve, but tonight hosted just Norbert, Nuts, Lily and Stew. An extra table setting sat empty.

“I suppose you haven't eaten much since you've been on the run?” Stew asked.

Nuts sprinkled salt onto the back of her hand and licked it off.

“You would be correct,” she said. “How long is dinner going to be?”

Lily tucked a napkin into her collar and slid the salt shaker back into the centre of the table. A few awkward minutes later, a server backed into the room with several bowls of ravioli, each one accompanied by a hunk of bread.

“Careful, you'll burn your...”

“Aaaagh!” cried Nuts, dangling her tongue into a glass of water.

“Are you okay?” Stew asked.

“Yeah, fine,” Nuts said. She wiped her face on her arm, put another piece of ravioli into her mouth and screamed again.

"Is that one going spare?" she said, pointing to the fifth table setting.

Lily nodded to Stew, who opened the door.

"Hi guys," said Anna, with a little wave. Her school uniform had been cleaned and pressed, and her hair brushed in an immaculate bob.

She rushed over to Norbert and hugged him, which took him by surprise since the last time they had seen her, she said he had ruined her life.

"Ah. The three young Rebels reunited," said Lily. "I hope your journey was not too...discombobulating."

Anna pulled out her chair and sat down, noticing immediately that she was the only one without bread. She took the second one from Nuts' side plate.

"I don't appreciate being bundled into a bag. But still, I never thought I'd be glad to see these two."

Nuts raised her eyebrows, cheeks stuffed.

'Well, maybe not you," Anna said quickly.

"Where to begin?" Lily said. "First Norbert, tell me where you are from? My spies tell me almost nothing about you that I can't tell by looking at you."

Norbert looked nervously at Nuts, and answered truthfully.

"I don't know. It all started when Baz - he's a demolition worker - found me in the basement of a house he was knocking down for the city. He took me home, and..."

"Why were you in the basement?" Lily asked as she ate.

"I don't know. I can vaguely remember running away from school, Blackstone High, but I'm starting to wonder if I dreamed that."

"Norbert, there is no Blackstone High," Stew chimed in.

Norbert smiled apologetically. "It's near Carston City."

"The one which was destroyed two decades ago?" Lily asked with a frown.

"Seventeen years," Anna said. "I know my history."

"Yes, that one," Norbert said.

Lily set down her fork. "Norbert, even if you did run away from a school that doesn't exist and magic your way through a wall, how did you end up in a basement? On top of a basement is a house, so you must have broken into it. Can you remember doing that?"

Norbert sighed, but was not able to answer this.

"They do have a history of break-ins, these two," Anna added. She moved her chair slightly closer to Lily.

"When were you found in the basement, Norbert?" asked Stew.

Nuts finished her meal. "It was Sunday. I remember because we couldn't call the city to find out who you were. The headquarters was shut."

Lily thought about this for a moment. "Okay it's possible then, that building was demolished during the week, and you fell into that exposed basement on Friday."

Norbert shrugged, and Lily nodded so that he would continue his story.

"So I lived at Baz's house for a few days. Kara - Nuts' mum - asked around in the missing persons department in the city headquarters and nobody my age has been reported missing. I think that's because my parents aren't around. Well..." Norbert looked down at his plate, and put down his fork. "They're even more missing than me."

Nuts put her arm around him.

"I'm sorry to hear that, mate," said Stew. "We know how it feels. All of us in this place have lost loved ones."

The group had emptied their bowls, except for Norbert. He exhaled slowly as his mum had once taught him to do when he was feeling anxious, then continued.

"After a few days at Baz's house I discovered the television could receive a channel that showed Beast Battle. Do you know about that?"

Lily and Stew looked at each other with narrowed eyes.

"Beast Battle? What is that?" asked Lily.

"Exactly," Norbert replied. "It's a sport which doesn't exist in Puzzle Forest, or if it does then it's kept secret. Huge robot animals beat each other up. Baz and I didn't know if it was pre-recorded from before Puzzle Forest, or if it's happening outside the city."

"Outside? We don't believe that rubbish here," she said firmly. "It's most likely a television channel which only very important members of the security council have access to. That wouldn't surprise me. Quite where they would hide an arena, though. Was it outdoors?"

The three kids nodded.

"Norbert, there are some people who believe there's life outside the wall," Lily said. "We call them Outsiders, and occasionally one of them will escape and never be seen again. There are people who believe the Earth is flat, too."

Nuts could tell this was a point of friction in the group, and asked, "What do you believe, Stew?"

"As a whole, the Rebels believe there's no life beyond the wall," he said diplomatically.

"Finally," Anna said. "I've been saying this for days."

Norbert told them about how he had wanted to find the source of the signal, and that had led them to the top of the antenna, and then onto the wall. Lily and Stew had long stopped eating by the time he recounted their experience inside the jail, and how they made it back into Puzzle Forest and went on the run.

"In the twelve years we have survived down here in the base, not one of us has entered the wall. That is really a remarkable, and incredibly dangerous feat," Lily said.

"Oh yeah, we saw Trixie too, twice," Nuts added, nonchalantly. "First when we went back to the destroyed house, and again when science boy was off on his antenna mission. Me and Anna were under the bed at Baz's flat when she shot two Hawks."

Lily and Stew nearly fell off their chairs in shock. Lily turned to Anna to corroborate. "Is this true?"

Anna nodded. She seemed shaken at the recollection of that fateful day. "We were under the bed. We saw the Beast Battle, too."

A server came to collect the plates and Nuts waited eagerly for a dessert which never came.

Stew looked at Lily, who nodded her approval. He looked Norbert in the eye.

"Norbert, I have some bad news. Baz didn't make it. Our sources inside the prison said he was executed by the Hawks."

Norbert's face went white, and Nuts jumped up and put her arms around him.

"It's not your fault, Norbert," she said, as tears silently rolled down his face. "It's not your fault."

"How can Lily be so sure?" Anna asked, smoothing out the sheet on Norbert's mattress. "I know Baz broke the rules with the television but surely that's not reason enough to...you know."

"Don't you get it?" Nuts said. "It's not because he broke the rules by adjusting his television. It's because they couldn't risk him telling anybody what he saw. The Beast Battle must prove that there's life outside, otherwise why kill him over it?"

"Don't tell me, the moon is made of cheese, too," she argued. "The signal for that channel could be coming from the same place that the regular TV channel comes from."

"No," Norbert said. He had barely spoken since dinner and his voice was croaky from crying. "I built the radioscope to measure the intensity of the signal. It's coming from outside the wall and it must have a power supply. One possibility is that it is solar powered and simply never stopped running. Or, more likely, there is life out there."

"There's no way there is life outside. Otherwise, why would Trixie have built it?" Anna asked.

Nuts hopped down from the top bunk and sat by Norbert, who was still on the edge of his bed and fighting back the tears.

"It's not your fault, Norbert," Nuts said.

"She's right, you know." Anna said, surprising everyone, including herself. She continued fussing with the sheets on her own bed. "Trixie and the Hawks - they do terrible things. They can make people do terrible things."

"How could it be anybody else's fault but my own? Baz was living happily, with a job and friends and a flat. Then I turned up and ruined everything. I remember seeing that cable tie inside his television, and I just *had* to snip it to find out what it did."

Norbert shook his head so vigorously that Nuts grabbed it and pulled it into her shoulder.

"Anybody else would have just put it back together," he continued. "But

I had to meddle with it, and now he's dead. So please don't say it's not my fault."

Norbert pulled away from Nuts and drew a sheet over himself. Nuts looked over at Anna, who had nothing more to say, so she blew out the candles and the three of them went to sleep listening to the sound of Norbert's sniffles.

Chapter 40

"I've stolen loads of stuff."

B reakfast at the base was a lively affair, in a long underground room with a seemingly endless table down the centre. Workers scurried in all directions, bumping each other with steaming bowls of porridge and mugs of coffee. The air was thick and the smells overpowering. Norbert's mind darted back to the dark days of Blackstone High. There, he avoided the chaos altogether, and simply waited out the lunch break in the toilets.

"Are you okay?" Anna asked.

He nodded, took a tray from a stack and lined up behind Nuts.

"I'm fine, it just reminds me of school," Norbert said.

"You recognise it, don't ya?" said a friendly voice. A man ahead of them in the queue had a bushy grey moustache and a broad, hunched back. He slid his tray along, but continued to chat to the newcomers.

"I'm Albo. I dig the tunnels. Well, not on me own, mind. With the other diggers of course. Anyway it's from the school."

The youngsters looked up at him, confused. In front of them was an unappetising vat of creamy white porridge, a few apples and some cereal.

"The slop! That's what I'm talking about. I said you probably recognise it, because it's from the school. That's where we rob it from. Ain't like you can grow stuff underground, so we have to go get it."

Norbert gave a polite smile and filled a bowl with corn flakes. Anna carefully inspected all the apples, and Nuts took a single grape and drowned it in honey. Albo chuckled.

"Here, come sit with me," he said. "I'll explain how this place works."

He loped off, checking behind him now and then to ensure that the three newcomers were following. He swung a leg over the bench and tapped the table, his fingernails thick with dirt.

"There are hundreds of us. Now and then one of us gets captured or killed in the line of duty - rest in peace - and there are new Rebels joining all the time. Like you guys. People who have discovered the truth about this place and want to live outside the rules."

He chugged a cup of black coffee and sighed, clearly enjoying the subterranean life.

"The Rebel base is a cobweb of tunnels under the city. Digging them out and making sure they don't collapse is my department."

"So this food, these tables, these chairs...where is it all from?" Anna asked.

"Robbed, of course," Albo said breezily. He shovelled in a mouthful of porridge.

Stealing food was a crime so serious in Puzzle Forest that even the theft of an apple could result in dire consequences. Anna struggled to take the first bite.

"So, this is what becomes of you when you fight the system and see the truth. You become a thief. You must be very proud of that," she Anna coldly.

"Not necessarily. There's five departments in this place. Homemaking. That's keeping the place nice and preparing the meals. Tunnelling. That's my bag, mostly done by people who know about construction. Procurement. That's the team who go up through the tunnels and into buildings, to get stuff - food, tools, timber, whatever. Then there's espionage. They get information by a network of informants who work for the city but feed information to us. That's the most dangerous of all. Then of course, there's Leadership. They keep everything running right."

Anna rolled her eyes at the idea of this bunch of parasites beneath Puzzle Forest, giving nothing back to the city she loved. Meanwhile Nuts was bouncing on the bench excitedly.

"Where do I sign?" she asked. "I want to do procurement. I've stolen loads of stuff. I stole a soldering iron once."

Albo laughed. "It's up to Lily. She will decide what you do in due course. For now, just get a sense of how this place works, and try to relax. Later on, you'll probably get given your roles."

Chapter 41

"There's no roof."

N uts, Anna and Norbert spent the day exploring. For ease of navigation, the labyrinth of tunnels was marked by road signs stolen from the world above. 'Puzzle Forest Public Library' indicated a small nook with a handful of dog-eared books. 'Central Hospital' was a multi-room suite in which seven Rebel babies had been born. The newcomers weren't allowed inside because they were too muddy. 'Central Highway' cut through the oversized rabbit warren, and was one of the few thoroughfares wide enough for the trio to walk side by side.

After lunch they were called to meet Lily in her chamber, where she sat on her raised plinth. Her skin was ghostly white and Norbert wondered if it was makeup or the ravages of a life without sunlight.

"I trust Stew is looking after you well," she said.

"Will I be getting my own room? I've never had to share before," said Anna, defiantly.

"No. Any other questions?" she replied. They shook their heads.

"You've probably been wondering what team you will be joining here in the Rebel base. I will tell you now," Lily said, clearly taking pleasure from the power she held in that room.

"Anna, you will be in Housekeeping."

"What?" Anna said indignantly. "Because I'm a girl? Unbelievable."

"Oh, please," Lily countered. "As a leader for over ten years, and a female, I find that rather insulting. No, you're in housekeeping because I can't trust you to do anything else. All the other roles require leaving the base and encountering citizens of Puzzle Forest. Right now I'm not convinced you would keep your mouth shut if you were threatened by an enemy, and until I become convinced of that you will stay underground. Is that understood?"

Anna smiled bitterly, unable to contain anger and disappointment.

"Nuts, you will join the procurement department. The 'scouts', as they call themselves. That team is led by Liberty, who I will introduce you to."

Nuts bopped her heels together and did a salute.

"And finally Norbert. You will be joining me in the leadership team."

Anna's jaws nearly hit the floor at this announcement. Nuts threw an arm around Norbert's shoulder, but he gnawed nervously at the inside of his mouth.

"What's the matter? Cat got your tongue?" Lily joked. "We were extremely impressed with your science skills at creating the television detector, and think you could bring valuable knowledge to our operation at the highest level. Nobody here understands science. Four electricians have lost their lives down here, trying to keep the lights on."

He sheepishly looked up at her and began to speak.

"I appreciate the thought. Especially considering you don't really know me. It's just, I..."

He swallowed, and looked round at Nuts, as his eyes welled up.

"I am going to leave Puzzle Forest and find my real home. I need to see if my parents have returned."

"Don't do it, Norbert! We can finally do some good in here," Nuts argued emphatically.

Lily stepped down from her throne and approached Norbert, placing a cold, bony hand on his forehead to test the temperature.

"Have you gone mad, child? You'll die out there of radiation. You'll be frazzled like a crisp, your body turned inside out by the rays," she said.

"I just...don't believe that," he said honestly. "I have been on top of the wall, and looked out. I didn't see any evidence of deadly radiation."

"Did you see any evidence of life?" Her voice was louder now, and ruffled.

"I saw trees," he said.

"And did you see animals? Did you see cities? Did you see roads and paths and buildings?" she asked, pacing around the room.

"No, I did not," Norbert said truthfully. "But I was only on the wall for a couple of minutes."

"Surely a clever boy like you knows that radiation is an invisible killer. You must know that radiation is a fact and not something one can simply argue doesn't exist," she continued.

Norbert half closed his eyes. "You know there's radiation in this room, right?"

"Don't be ridiculous. We're safe down here. We've lived here for years." she said, folding her arms.

"You radiate heat. That's radiation. Light coming from that candle is radiating towards our eyes and harmlessly bouncing off. Radiation from the sun keeps us alive. So yes, I know there's radiation outside the walls because there's radiation everywhere."

Lily returned to her throne and fanned herself. She looked nervously at a candle, flickering in an enclave in the wall.

"Well, go on," she said, irritably.

"Radiation just means energy travelling away from its source. Most of it is harmless and useful, like the sun's rays or radio waves. Long wavelengths."

Norbert motioned with his fingertip, slowly rising and falling as he rotated, drawing long S shapes across the air.

"The stuff you have to worry about is short wavelength." Now his fingertip was motioning up and down rapidly. "Gamma radiation. That might come from a bomb, or a power generating plant that exploded."

A self-satisfied smile returned to Lily's face.

"I see, so radiation *is* harmful and you were being pedantic. How helpful, Norbert," she said.

"Like I said, most radiation is harmless, but some is harmful. But here's why I'm not worried about going outside these walls. Firstly, what's the source of this small wavelength radiation? Puzzle Forest has been here for decades. If there was a radiation leak from a bomb or power plant in the first place 20 or 30 years ago, it would have dissipated by now."

"Dissipated?" Lily asked.

"Think about the way sound radiates from your mouth. It gets quieter, the further it travels. You can make it last a little longer by making it echo in a cave, but it doesn't last forever. That's the same for even harmful radiation."

Lily was now looking at the wall of her room, stunned by the revelation that they might have been hiding underground for the last twelve years for no reason.

"You said there 'firstly'. Is there a secondly?" she asked, finally.

"Yes. Secondly, there's no roof. Thinking walls keep you safe is like wearing a raincoat and expecting your hair to stay dry."

The room fell quiet as Lily, Nuts and Anna processed this bombshell. Nuts was the first to break the silence. She burst out laughing and jumped up, grabbing Norbert by the fingertips and dancing around him.

"So, we're free? I mean, we can just escape this place and explore the world?"

Norbert shrugged awkwardly.

"I'm thirteen years old and I don't even know where I live. But that's my theory, and I'm willing to bet my life that I'm right."

Nuts hugged him, then froze.

"Mum," she said, pulling away from Norbert and slumping back onto her seat. "I can't leave my mum. Being underground is one thing, but at least I could visit her somehow. Going over the top, that's so...final. I don't know, Norbert."

"Well I think the whole thing is ridiculous," Anna said, arms crossed. "If there wasn't radiation, there wouldn't be walls. Trixie wouldn't have built a city for no reason, so quite clearly you - a THIRTEEN YEAR OLD - might not have all the facts. Now if you'll excuse me I'll be returning to my quarters. I have to find a dustpan and brush and prepare for my new life, sweeping up mud. Whoopee."

With that, she left, slamming the door behind her. Lily sighed.

"Norbert, you are a smart boy, there's no denying that," she said. "Your scientific know-how could help us. Unfortunately, you cannot do that if you are dead. Now, this isn't a prison, and you are free to leave if that's what you want. But why don't you remain here for a week, so we can learn from you before you go. How does that sound?"

He looked at Nuts, who clasped her hands together.

"Okay. One week," he said.

Chapter 42

"Your jumps were a brush with death."

Anna reluctantly donned an apron and joined the cooks who prepared the meals. Within a few days she had alphabetised the spice cupboard and implemented an unpopular food hygiene protocol. Showers were a rarity beneath the ground, and the quality of food noticeably improved once the cooks had to cover their hair. Despite her growing sense of importance, she hated her new job. Or so she said.

Liberty was a reformed Hawk (like Stew) who seemed apprehensive about having Nuts join her group. Unlike most of the ragtag residents of the Rebel base, she dressed smartly and acted as if her job as lead scout was a proud career choice. She collected Norbert and Nuts from their quarters and led them to the hallowed map room, where a map of Puzzle Forest was carved into a wooden drum.

Norbert leaned over to read street names so small they must have been scored with a scalpel. The map undulated slightly where sandpaper had been used to erase sections which needed to be redrawn. Nuts ran her fingers over the surface, but Liberty quickly lifted her fingers away.

"Nuts, the initiation for joining the scouts is to copy the map. We have a thin sheet of paper which you will lay on top of the original, to trace every road, building and tunnel. It takes a long time. Days, sometimes weeks. There will be times when you consider missing out sections just to get it finished, but that won't do. You must copy it like your life depends on it, because one day it might. There are three reasons we copy the map. Firstly, it forces you to learn it."

Liberty held out her hand, palm facing down.

"This is the surface of Puzzle Forest."

Her other palm joined it from below.

"This is our network of tunnels. You must know how it all interacts, and drawing out the map will force you to learn it."

Nuts nodded, eager to crack on with her homework, for the first time in her life.

"Secondly, this map needs to be precious to you, because you will need to protect it with your life. If the Hawks ever find a copy of this map, it will lead them straight to our bases and be the end of the resistance. If they capture you, we lose a Rebel. If they capture this map, we lose everything."

Nuts swallowed, understanding the scale and importance of the task ahead.

"What's the third reason?" she asked.

"We don't have a printer. I recommend you start in the centre and work your way out, so you don't smudge the work you've already done. Good luck young lady. Once your map is complete, we can lacquer it to lock the pencil markings in place."

Liberty exited the room and left Norbert and Nuts to it. They carefully lifted a sheet of paper from a wide wooden drawer and carried it to the table, laying it onto the map. Nuts clipped it to the wooden table all the way around while Norbert sharpened a couple of pencils until the points were like pins. Nuts climbed onto the wooden table, and began to outline the City Headquarters building. Norbert set about tracing the industrial district which contained the antenna.

Over the coming days, they filled in the vast and detailed map, line by line. Pencils were slowly ground down to stubs, as the two kids tried to make sense of the world.

"What was your dad like, Norbert?" Nuts asked, one afternoon. The room was empty and quiet, aside from the noise of pencils sliding over the thin paper.

"He taught physics, and..."

Nuts already looked confused.

"Planets, forces. All that stuff," Norbert said. "My dad loved puzzles and riddles. My mum too, was super smart."

"What sort of thing did you do, though?" Nuts asked. "What was your house like?"

Norbert put down his pencil and sat back on a wooden chair, deep in thought.

"I remember the last Christmas we spent together. We carried a tree back to the house, me at the light end, Dad at the other. Base first through the front door so it didn't snap the branches. Mum was making dinner and I can still smell the nut loaf if I really close my eyes and concentrate. Dad could barely lift me to put on the tree topper because I was ten and getting too big for that."

Nuts noticed Norbert's eyes welling up, and came over to comfort her friend. "Is that your last memory of them? What happened?" Nuts asked.

"No, but that's a nice memory. The last time I saw them was when I was packing for Space Camp. It was my parent's anniversary, and while I was away they went off on an aeroplane for a two night holiday."

Norbert thumbed the sharp tip of his pencil. He breathed in deeply and blinked away the tears.

"On Sunday night I got dropped off back home. They weren't there. I made dinner and assumed their flight was delayed. The next day, I didn't know what to do, so I went to school as normal. But when I got home from school they still weren't there. Their plane had crashed into the ocean, and there were no survivors. Well, that's what the newspaper said, but I didn't believe it. Still don't believe it."

His voice was barely audible now and he struggled to get the words out.

"There's no evidence that my parents are dead. Only that they are missing," he said. "And I made a model which proved they could have survived."

"Did your grandparents look after you after your parents disappeared?" Nuts asked.

"No, but I told the school that my grandma had moved in with me, and I kept going to school. I knew my mum's bank account number, for food deliveries. I didn't tell the teachers because at first I thought they'd be home any day. As the weeks passed, I knew that if I told the school the truth, they would put me in an orphanage or put me in somebody else's home. So I just pretended everything was fine, and I lived alone. Well, me and Owly."

"For how long?" asked Nuts.

"A year and a bit. I've had two Christmasses without them."

Norbert looked up at Nuts, and wiped the tears from his face. "That's why I need to get out of here. They might be back. They might be home."

Nuts nodded. "What's Christmas? Is it like Trixmas?"

Norbert dropped his head into his hands.

"Aagh. I have to get out of here, Nuts. It's insane. What about your dad? What happened to him?"

"He was gone by the time I was five, and I don't really remember him. Mum never speaks much about Dad, and I don't ask her because it upsets her. I get the impression he was brave and courageous, but she never tells me what she means by that. I suppose he was an adrenaline junkie like me, doing stunts. Sucks we never got to BASE jump together, I reckon he'd have loved that. It's the ultimate rush, Norbert."

"It's awful, Nuts. You very nearly splatted on the beach when you jumped out of that tree. Then you nearly hit a wall when we jumped off that antenna. Both of your jumps were a brush with death."

Nuts smiled and soaked up the memory like a ray of sunlight breaking through dark thunderclouds. They stood, and unexpectedly, Nuts threw her arms around Norbert.

"Don't leave, Norbert," she said. "Your family is here now. I used to wish my dad would come walking through the door, every night. But really, if their plane crashed into the ocean and you haven't heard from them in years, it does sound like they might be gone."

Norbert shook his head.

"They're not dead. They can't be. Nuts you're the best - well maybe the only - friend I've ever had, apart from Owly. And if I can't find my family, I'll come back. I promise."

Nuts returned to the table. She sighed, and sharpened her pencil for the hundredth time that day.

"You don't get it, Norbert. That's what everyone's trying to tell you. There is no coming back."

A tear dropped onto her map, soaking into the paper.

"Not you as well!" he said, passing her a balled-up tissue. "I thought you believed me when I said the radiation outside should be fine?"

Nuts sniffled. "I don't know what to believe."

Chapter 43

"Can't we just hack it?"

With a lot of help from Norbert, Nuts completed her map over two long days. Liberty sprayed it with a special lacquer which prevented the pencil lines from smudging, and showed Nuts how to fold it down into her backpack. It was a work of art, with the street names written so small that Nuts had to bring the map to her nose to read them. Again Liberty gave Nuts the lecture about how it was more valuable than her own life, and she must be willing to die to protect their underground location. She told him of a Rebel who was once caught with her map and ate the entire thing while she was in the back of the Hawk's car.

Nuts' first mission was to her former school, which meant trekking for miles through a maze of concrete pipes. Water ran down the gulley between her feet, and Nuts had to keep swapping sides to dodge it. Her partner in crime was a teenager who had spent most of her life underground, and went by the nickname Fox. She had a shaved head, fingerless gloves and a spiked leather jacket.

"What's your real name?" Nuts asked.

"You don't need to know," Fox replied.

"I'm not going to snitch. Whatever," Nuts said.

"You're a newcomer. Until you've proven yourself, you're not to be trusted."

Fox lifted a set of bars from a wall and crawled into a pipe so narrow that she had to drag her backpack behind her. The duo were covered in mud by the time they reached a chamber with a wooden floorboard overhead.

"This is it," Fox said. "We're directly beneath the kitchens of the school."

They unscrewed a wooden plank and cautiously pulled themselves up through the hole. Being the middle of the night, the school was empty and the pair made quick work of filling their backpacks with the items on the list.

"Why do we need cinnamon? What even is that?" tutted Fox, who searched the cupboards for a fussy list of ingredients.

Nuts found a large jar of cinnamon and tossed it into her bag. "Got it," she said.

Fox shook her head and took it out.

"If we take a whole jar, someone will notice that it disappeared. We have to put some of it into a new jar that I brought with me. Then next time, we hit another school or restaurant. Slow and steady wins the race."

Nuts nodded and spooned the cinnamon from one jar to the other, making sure not to spill any of the brown powder onto the floor.

Fox ran her finger down the list. With nothing left to get, she stuffed it into her backpack and drew the string tight. As she dropped back through the hole, Nuts stared out over the kitchen counter, where she had queued so many times for her lunch. She looked at the stack of red plastic trays and the posters of Trixie on the wall, and wondered if she would ever go to school again. A smile spread across her face. It was crime or prison from now on in, she thought.

Fox hurried her to jump down through the floorboards and the two returned to the base. Their work was finished at four-o-clock in the morning and Nuts slept in until lunch.

"Living the dream," she yawned as she awoke.

Meanwhile, Norbert met with the leadership council. He took his seat at a large, wooden table, whose boards were a bumpy mishmash of planks. Everything in the base was recycled or upcycled or simply stolen. It felt, to Norbert, like an animal's burrow crossed with a doll's house.

Around the table sat Stew, Liberty and four people Norbert had not yet met. The adults made small talk about broken water pumps and cold nights. Lily eventually swanned in with her trademark white makeup and dark eye shadow, which reminded Norbert of a raccoon. She whispered to a server who stood by the door, and took her seat. As she introduced the meeting, the assistant worked his way around the room, blowing out the candles.

Glasses of red wine were handed out. One of the ladies smiled at Norbert and said "Perhaps you'd prefer an orange squash."

Before he could answer, Lily began.

"Welcome Norbert, to the Leadership Council. Let me introduce everyone. Liberty and Stew, you know. This is Sioux who leads the housekeeping department. Harper, who looks after engineering. You two should get on well."

Harper tucked her napkin into her neckline and ignored the introduction. A bland potato soup was served and classical music played from speakers buried into the mud walls.

"So, I heard you don't believe in radiation," Harper said, taking the trouble to set down her spoon to do air quotes around 'believe'.

"Now, now, Harper," added Sioux. "It's not that he doesn't *believe* in it, he just thinks his youthful looks will protect him."

The adults sniggered and Norbert felt as if he'd stumbled into the staff room at Blackstone High.

"It's his big brain," Liberty exclaimed, her cheeks glowing from the wine. "It's a radiation shield!"

They howled with laughter and Norbert squirmed in his chair. The only one not laughing was Stew, who looked embarrassed.

"I tell you what though, young man," said Sioux. "I do admire your conviction. I mean, I've heard people before question whether the radiation is as lethal as Trixie claims, but none of them really believed their own nonsense. If they did, they'd get over that wall and prove it."

"Well, if he's wrong about it, he can always come back," said Harper. "Oh no, just kidding. He'll be burned up and churned up. Upside down and inside out."

"Come on now," Stew said. "It's his first, and maybe only time here. Let's show Norbert what he'll be missing, not humiliate him."

Harper, Sioux and the others glanced at each other between mouthfuls of the soup, but the meal continued without any more teasing. Norbert thought about the source of the Beast Battle channel and the many reasons he had told Lily why radiation can't exist. But the moment had passed and it was too late to defend himself. The attitude of the leadership council only strengthened his resolve to escape Puzzle Forest, come what may. Adults, he thought, could be as mean as kids.

There was talk of business, as each of the leaders updated Lily with their latest news. Liberty said that the Shadow Runners event was coming up on the weekend, and that gave them a fantastic opportunity to raid for materials they could only find in the city headquarters.

Stew could see that Norbert was lost.

"Shadow Runners is an annual event in Puzzle Forest. You must have forgotten it because you would have seen it when you were growing up. There's one morning a year where the sun is so low in the sky that it casts the antenna's shadow onto the inside of the wall. It's the only time of year that inhabitants are allowed out into the forest and be near the perimeter. At five o'clock there are crowds of people by ladder 343, and race the shadow until about ten o-clock in the morning when the sun gets too high. It's fun seeing everyone jog through the trees. I used to love it when I was, you know, on the other side."

"Most importantly," Liberty added. "All of the Hawks are out by the wall policing the event, so we do an annual raid on the city headquarters. Some provisions can only be found there."

Norbert nodded. "Sounds dangerous. Nuts will like that. What items do you need from there?"

"It's a calculated risk," Liberty said. "After you three confirmed our suspicion that vast numbers of prisoners are being kept inside the wall, we decided to find a list of names of those held captive."

"Norbert, over the years we've had dozens of our members captured by Hawks," Lily added. "We always assumed they had been shot, and held funerals. It's possible though, that at least some of them are alive inside that prison. So I have asked Liberty to infiltrate the headquarters and find out who made it."

"Won't the list be held on a server?" Norbert asked. "Can't we just hack it?"

The leadership council looked at each other with total confusion.

"Servers are for wine, young man," Liberty said. "If a list exists, it will be kept in a filing cabinet in an archive room. Call us old-fashioned, Norbert but when we need a list, we get paper and pen and write one. We don't understand the words you are using."

Norbert nodded and gave up on his line of questioning. The others talked among themselves about their various missions, and Norbert kept looking at the door, hoping the server would return to take everyone's plates.

He cast his mind back to the day he woke up in the basement and tried to recall seeing any computers in his entire time in Puzzle Forest. The most sophisticated technology he had seen was a television, and even that had to warm up before the colours looked right. Norbert's childhood home had been packed with electronics, from radio controlled planes to automatic lighting. Even the coffee machine knew to automatically start brewing when his parents awoke. He couldn't understand how he had gone from a world awash with technology to a place as backward as Puzzle Forest, and wondered, not for the first time, if he had travelled back in time. He didn't believe in time travel, but knew that a good scientist keeps all possibilities alive until they are proven to be dead. Also, he was sure that Trixie had a smartphone, when he saw her at Puzzle Manor.

Norbert was awoken from his dreamlike daze when Stew nudged him, and said it was time to leave. The council were thanking Lily for another excellent dinner. Norbert politely nodded to his company and returned to his bunk room, more eager than ever to escape the city and see if normality lay beyond. He felt sure he would lose his mind if he stayed underground another day.

Chapter 44

"It's a message for me."

Anna's bunk was already empty when Norbert and Nuts awoke. Within one week of being in the Rebel base, Anna had been promoted to senior breakfast chef and was now bossing the adults around at six o-clock in the morning. Nuts hung her head over the top bunk and watched Norbert drop his few belongings into his backpack. A torch. The purple blanket he had been given by Baz. A wingsuit, freshly repaired, to get from the antenna to the top of the wall.

"I'll come with you. Not over the wall, but to the antenna," Nuts said.

Norbert shook his head.

"What if you get caught?" he said. "Then you'll become yet another casualty of being around me. Stay home and eat the porridge. The further you get away from me, the safer you'll be. I will miss you though. So much."

"No, really. I know some great short cuts that'll get us most of the way underground. Then we can emerge under one of the city buildings when it's closed, and walk the rest of the way through alleyways and gardens. If there is any sign of a Hawk, I'll split and you're on your own. Don't worry about me."

"Okay, thanks Nuts."

Norbert said farewell to a few Rebels he had befriended. He knocked on Lily's door, and entered when called.

"So, you're really doing this?" Lily said. "You know you've got slim to no hope of getting to the base of that antenna without being spotted, let alone to the top. If you somehow manage it, you'll have to survive a ridiculous skydive to the wall. Assuming the guard towers aren't staffed, then you have another leap to the outside. Where, of course, you'll be frazzled. When it happens, don't say I didn't tell you so."

Norbert half closed his eyes and said "Well if I'm dead, I won't be able to say anything at all."

Lily smirked but Norbert wasn't joking. He knew there was a chance she was right. But he couldn't shake the feeling that somewhere outside of Puzzle Forest, his parents were looking for him. He had to get back to his real home, with its apple tree and Owly. One of the few things he was sure of, was that home was not inside the wall.

"Well, thanks for having me," he said, as if he was thanking a friend's mum at the end of a play date. Lily held the door open, and that was as much warmth as she could muster. She looked down the hallway to check they were not being overheard.

"Norbert," she whispered, her eyes locking onto his. "Don't come back."

After lunch, Norbert and Nuts left the base via a disused sewage pipe tall enough to stand in. Now and then they stopped to look at the map Nuts had brought with her, but for the most part, the byways underneath Puzzle Forest had become as familiar as the woods beyond the tower blocks.

"Will you ever try to visit your mum?" Norbert asked.

"Of course," Nuts said. "I think about her every day. But not yet. I need to build up some trust here first. If I get busted speaking to someone up above, I'd never be allowed back in the base."

After several hours of travel, Nuts announced that they had reached their destination. She carefully removed a floorboard from the ceiling and the duo squeezed up through the hole. It was a warehouse containing road signs, traffic lights and diggers. A muddy pickaxe reminded Norbert of Baz, and the thought of his old friend sent a shiver down his spine.

Norbert and Nuts had surfaced in an industrial district scattered with warehouses and chain link fences. It was as close as Nuts could get to the hill on which the antenna was placed. Now in an unmanned storage depot, a window cast a beam of sunlight across the dusty concrete floor. Nuts opened it and climbed through, ushering Norbert to join her outside.

They crept from building to building, sticking to the shadows and crawling across the ground where there was no cover. Peeking out from behind a storage shed, they spotted a Hawk patrolling the road that ran up to the antenna. A stun gun swung at his thigh as he paced forward and back.

"It's no good, Norbert," Nuts whispered. "Let's go inside and look at the map. There must be another approach."

Nuts inserted a paperclip into the lock and wriggled open. The two kids slipped into a dark shed full of yellow signs warning of radiation and featuring the grim image of a skull. Nuts pulled the precious map from her backpack and examined the area around the antenna.

"If we go back underground and use this tunnel, we can resurface to the west of the tower in the CLIMB district. Then we'll work our way into the forest and up the hill."

Norbert nodded. "Okay. What's the CLIMB district?"

"Oh, I dunno what that area is really called. It's just the streets near the periphery road start with C - at Cocoa Avenue, then L, then I, M, B. I noticed it when I was copying out the map last week. So I call it the CLIMB district."

Nuts began to fold the map, but Norbert stopped her and smoothed it back open.

"That's a strange coincidence, isn't it? It spells out a word. What comes before and after it?"

"Nothing, just nonsense," Nuts said. "It's just coincidence that it spells a word."

Norbert crouched and looked carefully at this quiet corner of suburbia, and indeed saw the letters spelling CLIMB.

"Do you have a pencil?" he asked.

Nuts reached into her backpack and retrieved one, peeping out of the crack in the shed door for any signs of life outside.

"Norbert, we haven't really got time for this. Can we get out of here?" she asked.

"Just give me a minute. The next two streets are Indina Avenue and then Nightingale Lane. It spells CLIMB IN, but then it goes to a jumble of letters that don't seem to spell anything. SHDWATVII. Then there's a natural gap in the streets for a park."

"I did tell you it was nonsense," said Nuts. "Come on, let's get out of here!"

Norbert wrote the names of the streets around the word CLIMB IN. His strip of paper said:

LSTATXIII CLIMB IN SHDWATVII.

He stuffed the strip of paper into his backpack and followed Nuts out of the door, which she carefully locked. They returned to the road sign warehouse and dropped down through the floorboards to the safety of the tunnels.

"Okay, so now we go west a bit," Nuts said. "We'll come up right near the edge of the forest and work our way back in, towards the antenna. I'm hoping that there won't be any guards on that side."

Norbert nodded but his mind was on the letters STATX, which he kept reading over and over again.

"Are you alright, Norbert? I know you're scared but remember, you've done this before."

They stopped for water, leaning back against the damp tunnel walls.

"Just climb it, no matter if they are shouting at you from below," Nuts said. "Same as before. Get to the top then glide. Hopefully the wind will take you right over it this time."

Norbert nodded, unsure if the tunnel was incredibly hot or he was sweating out of fear of what was to come.

"What was the leadership meeting like?" Nuts asked, changing the subject.

"Oh. Erm, well they all seem to know what they're doing. Liberty mentioned that she had a new recruit and you were doing well. Mostly they're planning for the Shadow Runners event. I'm probably not meant to tell you this, but they're going to do a raid on the city headquarters while all the Hawks are distracted by policing the race."

"Sweet!" Nuts said. "Did they say if I was on the team going into the city headquarters? Norbert? Norbert?"

He was staring at the strip of paper again.

"SHDW could mean SHADOW. 'Climb in Shadow'. Can I borrow your pencil again?"

Norbert wrote out:

LSTATXIII. Climb in Shadow. ATVII

"Maybe the first part is irrelevant. Looks like STATX and all I can think is about static electricity," he said.

Nuts put her hand on his shoulder.

"Mate, you need to focus on getting up that antenna, not on the names of roads in a place you'll never see again. Are you sure you want to do this today? It feels like your mind isn't on the job, and it's a *big* job."

"Nuts, why would the names of the streets have a message in them?"

She let out a weary sigh.

"Firstly, it might be coincidence. I spent three whole days copying out that map. There are thousands of streets in this city. Some of them are bound to form short words. Secondly, if it is a secret message, it's probably just the person whose job it is to name the streets got bored."

"You might be right, but there's something odd about it to me. This place is totally devoid of humour. The person who named the streets would not risk their life to insert a joke. If anything they'd just make them alphabetical, because that's the sort of soulless, methodical way things are done here."

"Hmm. Well, it could be a short word; AT," suggested Nuts, as she ran her fingers over the paper.

He amended his note to read:

"LST at XIII Climb in Shadow at VII."

The pencil dropped from his fingertip.

"Are you okay?" asked Nuts. "You look like you're going to be sick. Let's get out of this tunnel."

But Norbert didn't move. He slumped down onto the floor, a streamlet of muddy water soaking his jeans.

"It's a message," he said quietly. He swallowed, and looked at Nuts.

"It's a message for me."

Chapter 45

"I space out and chew crayons."

Norbert insisted they abandon the antenna escape plan, to give him time to get his head around the riddle he had discovered. Back in their bunk room, he explained to Nuts how Roman numerals worked, for the tenth time.

"So X means ten, and there are three ones after it. Therefore, thirteen," Norbert said.

"But why? Why not just say THIRTEEN."

Nuts was agitated and confused by this message. She wondered if the stress of escape had Norbert seeing things.

"The more cryptic the puzzle, the more likely nobody who works for the city is going to figure it out. It says Lost at Thirteen. Climb in the Shadow at Seven. I am thirteen and I'm lost. Could be coincidence, but it's too strange to dismiss."

Later that morning they spoke to Lily and Stew.

"This Roman thing. How do you know about this ancient language?" she asked.

"Everybody at school has to learn it. It's just common knowledge," Norbert answered.

"I vaguely remember it from the old world," Lily said. "Nuts, you went to school more recently than me; did they teach you this?"

"I don't think so. But normally I space out and chew crayons," she said.

"That makes me think that the message was aimed at me," Norbert said, excitedly.

"But it says 'lost at thirteen'," Lily pointed out, prowling around the room and looking at nothing in particular as she thought. "These roads were named twenty ago. We just had our anniversary celebrations. You weren't even born yet, so how would they anticipate that you would, in seven years time, be born. Then thirteen years later, you might become lost? Here."

Norbert slumped in his chair, stumped by this. It didn't make sense and deep down he knew that it was impossible. However, he also knew that some things don't make sense until you have the solution, and perhaps it required a whole new way of thinking.

"Suppose, somehow, the person who created the road names could see the future," Lily chuckled. "Then what do you think he or she is asking you to do?"

"I'm not sure about that either. But when I saw the word Shadow - well the S H D W which I assume means shadow, I thought about that meeting we had here where you talked about Shadow Runners. Can you explain that again please, Lily?"

Stew leaned forward on the sofa, getting a nod from Lily to proceed.

"Once a year, the sun is just low enough in the sky that in the morning it casts a shadow of the antenna onto the wall. From about 6 o'clock to lunchtime, it passes around the inside of the wall."

Norbert picked up the strip of paper with the riddle scrawled on it, grabbed a pencil, and then took a candle from an alcove. Returning to the table, he set the strip of paper on its side to make a long arc, like the wall.

"So this is the sun," he said, raising the candle in his left hand. "It throws a shadow onto the wall like this."

Norbert manoeuvred the candle closer to the pencil to cast a vertical shadow onto the paper representing the wall.

"As the sun moves, it will pass various ladders, right? At seven in the morning, once a year, one of the ladders is in the shadow. That's what it's asking me to climb."

He set down the pencil and returned the candle. The three others were now intrigued.

"That could be it!" Stew said, patting Norbert on the back. "Only one problem. It's also the one day of the year when the entire city is there, Hawks and all. Remember, at Shadow Runners they're trying to outrun the shadow so there will be thousands of people in those woods at the time. You'll get spotted the minute you put a hand on the first rung."

"Stew's right," Lily said. "It would be out of the question to get you into that crowd of runners. Your face is on posters all over the city. The place will be crawling with Hawks."

Nuts had an idea.

"What if Albo digs a tunnel that's not connected to the rest of the Rebel system, but just enough to get under that fence so Norbert doesn't have to climb it? Perhaps he could put a trapdoor in the woods, so Norbert can wait in the tunnel overnight and emerge at the base of the ladder just before seven. Then he can climb in the shadow right on time."

"All right, that sounds like the least terrible idea we have," said Lily. "I'll have Albo and his team get to it immediately. It's three days until the event, so the place will already be full of workers clearing the track and putting up fencing. They'll have to dig at night."

"How will you know which stairs the shadow will hit at seven?" Nuts asked.

"I'll work that out," said Norbert. "We'll go tomorrow morning, Nuts, and take some measurements. I think it'll be easy enough, since the ladders are spaced so far apart."

"The thing that worries me," Stew interjected, "Is that Hawks have guns. Just because you manage to start climbing, doesn't mean you'll make it to the top."

None of them had an answer for this, and on the sobering thought of Norbert falling from the the wall, the meeting was adjourned. Back in the bunk room, Anna thought it was the stupidest thing she had ever heard, and quickly turned the conversation to the fact she had won the Shadow Runners in the Under Eights's category a few years ago. Her mother had simply said 'Finally', and ushered her off to school.

The next day, Norbert and Nuts were up before dawn and scurried under the city to the western wall where the shadow would fall. They crept up through a trapdoor which was tucked into some woodland, and made the rest of the journey above ground in the cool night air. They made their way to the wall, and sat with their backs against a tree stump as the sun began to rise.

"I'm worried they're going to shoot you in the butt," Nuts said truthfully. "Is it too late to design you some metal pants?"

She laughed at her own joke.

"Brilliant. Thanks Nuts," Norbert smiled. "If I had them, I would wear them."

The glow of the sun emerged on the horizon, and the dark black shadow of the antenna fell across the wall. As the time approached seven o'clock, the sun's position had moved to where it was obvious which one would be in the shadow; ladder 347. They wrote it down, not that Norbert would forget, and made their way back to the Rebel base.

Chapter 46

"The cleverest fool I have ever known."

The night before Shadow Runners, Norbert was visibly nervous. He retied his laces several times, and even practised crawling from under the bunk bed and onto the ladder. Anna handed him a sandwich wrapped in brown paper and tied neatly with string. Despite having been at the rebel base for a few weeks, it was the first time he had seen her without her school uniform.

"When the Hawks beat the truth out of you, be sure to tell them I'm innocent," she smiled. Norbert chuckled, but Anna didn't. "I'm serious," she said.

Norbert shook Anna's hand, and apologised again for dragging her away from her perfect life.

"It wasn't so perfect," she admitted. "It's quite liberating to wake up here without my mother giving me a list of goals for the day."

Nuts handed Norbert a padlock, which was open.

"No key?" he said.

"Nah. It's for the gate on the enclosure by the wall. As soon as you emerge at the base of the ladder, lock the door with this padlock so the Hawks can't chase you up it."

Norbert carefully placed the padlock into the bag without squeezing it shut. He left the room and found the corridor outside was lined with characters from the rebel base. News of his escape plan had spread like wildfire, and the audaciousness of climbing a ladder in the middle of the biggest event in Puzzle Forest had made Norbert the ultimate rebel. They shook his hand eagerly and wished him luck.

"Good luck, fella," said Stew, warmly. "I am seriously worried you're going to die once you get outside that wall, but every finger and toe is crossed in the hope that you are right and all of us are wrong. If anyone can figure out life on the outside, it's you. Just promise me one thing, yeah?"

"What's that?" asked Norbert.

"You'll come back for us," he said.

Norbert nodded, and he wondered, as he had done for the last few days, why Lily had said the opposite. Perhaps she imagined that he might get followed, and give up the Rebel base for good.

Albo stood next to Stew, and explained that he had dug a short tunnel, disconnected from the main network.

"It goes from a great oak tree, under the road they've made, and up into the base of ladder 347. It's deep," he said. "Because there are tree roots everywhere.'

Norbert thanked him, and at the end of the line was Lily.

"You are a fool, Norbert. Perhaps the cleverest fool I have ever known. When they capture you, you tell them that you've been living in the woods alone, of course."

Norbert nodded, unsure how to take the backhanded compliment. He began walking down the corridor to rapturous applause. Nuts joined him, as once again she would escort Norbert to as close to ladder 347 as possible.

The two friends trekked through dark, muddy underpasses and some hours later they reached a junction.

"This is it, you gnarler," Nuts said, giving Norbert a hug. "Come and get me and my mum. Invent a flying machine or something and come scoop us up and take us to your new fortress or wherever you end up living. And the laser yo-yo. The world needs it."

"Definitely," Norbert promised.

He made his way through the hatch and into the dark night, being sure to keep his head torch off. The forest floor was quiet, as there was never much of a breeze in Puzzle Forest, especially this close to the wall. Norbert carefully made his way towards the enormous ladder he could see in the distance, soaring up endlessly out of view. As he approached, he saw that the road on which everyone would run was marked out by red tape. There were dozens of oak trees dotted around, but one stood out as being particularly large and Norbert scratched around at its base to find a hatch. He felt a hard surface beneath a scattering of leaves, and managed to pull up the wooden trapdoor. He squeezed into the hole feet first, and dropped the hatch back over his head.

The hole which Albo had dug was like a waterslide, sloping down in the direction of the wall. Norbert tumbled down on his back, and when the tunnel levelled out he managed to turn himself around and crawl head first. Eventually his head reached the exit hatch, which he tested. Good to his word, Albo had made it surface at the foot of ladder 347.

Norbert's mind was a cyclone of fearsome thoughts, circulating endlessly. He pictured the Hawks shooting at him. His body peeling away from the ladder and dropping like a stone. He imagined finally reaching the top, only to find a guard waiting for him and dragging him to an exercise bike in a dungeon. Worst of all, he couldn't shake the feeling that he might have miscalculated the risk of radiation. The images of mutant animals haunted his shivering, sleepless night.

After what felt like an eternity, his watch read six o'clock. Norbert heard a distant voice; a city worker, he assumed, setting up the event. Anna had described it in detail, and Norbert knew that tables would be unfolded and stocked with cups of water and warm cocoa before the event began. There would be photographers from the Puzzle Forest newspaper and film crews for the television station. As the minutes ticked forward, the din of voices and footsteps became louder until it was so thick with noise that Norbert felt like there was a riot going on above his head. Still he hid away from the world in a tiny hole, with a few planks of wood above his head.

'Climb in the shadow at seven' kept running through his mind. If he was right about the riddle, blowing this opportunity would mean waiting an entire year to try again.

At quarter to seven, the vibrations from runners shook the mud onto his shoulders and into his hair. He could now make out the conversations between runners, one of them shrieking with excitement about outrunning the shadow. It was time to climb in the shadow at seven, and find out what this riddle was all

Chapter 47

"Get down from there!"

Exhaling deeply to calm his nerves, Norbert popped open the hatch and emerged from the tunnel. Despite being in the shadow of the antenna, his eyes still had to acclimate to the morning light. A forest of legs thundered past his enclosure, which was an area about the size of a bed. Thankfully nobody seemed to notice him climb through the hatch and clip a padlock onto the gate.

Norbert gripped the first rung of the ladder and began to climb it. Adrenaline surged into his body as he purposefully stepped, rung after rung, past the height of the chain link fence. As the regularity of his movements became second nature, he looked up towards the top of the wall and gulped at the unbelievable distance ahead of him. There was no sign of the top, only a ladder that disappeared into a tiny speck. Looking back down, only the stragglers and parents with young children were walking by, resigned to being captured by the shadow. Within minutes, Norbert was at the height of the tree tops and his muscles began to ache. That's when the first shouts came from below.

"Hey, get down from there!"

He looked down and saw a Hawk with her hands cupped around her mouth. A handful of runners had also stopped to see what was going on. Norbert barely paused, and with new resolve he began to climb even faster.

"Get down immediately!" came a loud voice, now using a megaphone to reach Norbert. This attracted more runners, some of whom came back into the shadow to witness the fracas. A crowd gathered around the base of the ladder and two Hawks bashed away at the padlock with branches.

With sweaty palms making it ever harder to grip the rungs, Norbert continued to charge upwards.

"Norbert, we know who you are," came a new voice from the loudspeaker. "You will not survive the radiation. Do NOT continue. Return to the ground and we can talk."

The Hawks managed to smash through the padlock and one of them began to chase Norbert up the ladder. By this point he was well on his way, so high that the canopy of trees had merged into a continuous carpet of green. Heart pounding and sweat stinging his eyes, Norbert continued to surge skyward. At the base of the ladder, several Hawks now barked at the crowd to disperse, even thrashing at them with sticks.

"There is nothing here to see. You must leave or be arrested. Go! Now!" they screamed, shoving parents away from the scene.

A car drove along the track, its horn beeping continuously to force any remaining runners to jump out of the way into the bracken. It screeched to a halt at the base of the ladder and a Hawk emerged with a long, plastic case. She put it onto the back of the car and unclipped the hinges, opening it to reveal a rifle. Lifting it quickly and flicking down its legs, the gun was set up on the roof of the car and aimed almost vertically.

"This is Hawk 93113," the sharpshooter said over her radio. "I have the fugitive in my sights and need permission to shoot."

Horrified parents grabbed their children and bolted from the scene. But despite the best efforts from the Hawks, more passers-by gathered at the fence they had erected, desperate to find out what was going on.

"Permission granted. Fire when ready," came a reply over the radio.

The Hawk put her eye to the scope and her finger on the trigger.

"No you don't," screamed a voice, and at that moment a woman clambered onto the roof of the car.

Kara stood in front of the gun, blocking the muzzle with her chest.

"That boy is innocent and if you want to shoot him you'll have to shoot me first," she said.

"Get away from the gun, now! He is a wanted criminal, and we have orders to shoot."

"Well you have orders from me to not shoot," said Kara, gripping the barrel of the gun, her eyes tight shut.

"Madam, obstructing the work of a Hawk is a crime and we will arrest you if you do not move immediately," the Hawk shouted.

Kara refused to budge, and was dragged backwards by two Hawks. The sharpshooter put her eye to the scope and manoeuvred it back into place, almost vertically.

As her finger squeezed the trigger, Kara, held by her shoulders, kicked the gun with all her might and it clattered onto the floor, sending a bullet into the wall. Three Hawks stuffed her into the vehicle, telling her she was arrested for violations against a city officer. She just smiled as she heard the sharpshooter say:

"This is Hawk 93113. The fugitive has escaped out of range. Over."

At the top of the ladder, Norbert finally hauled himself onto the roof of the wall. He was exhausted from the epic climb and his heart beat like a drum. He lay on the gravel, unable to move until he caught his breath. He knew the Hawk chasing him was only a few minutes behind, and he had to regain his composure and leap from the wall to freedom.

As he rolled onto his front to stand, he saw a pair of black boots, and assumed that the worst had happened; a Hawk waiting for him on top of the wall. Norbert looked up, and saw that it was not a Hawk but an old man wearing goggles and a hooded jacket.

"Norbert, you're alive!" he said. "Come! We don't have much time."

The man reached out a hand and Norbert accepted it.

"Who are you? And where are we going?" Norbert asked. "Is there life outside the wall?"

The man pulled Norbert to his feet and paced backwards across the gravel. "There is life outside these walls. But not as you know it."

"Your voice," Norbert said, exhausted and confused. "Do I know you?"

The man moved his goggles onto the top of his head. Wisps of silver-white hair flailed in the wind. His cheeks were red, skin textured with age. His eyes were a soft blue, almost grey, and focused on Norbert with an intensity matched only by his electric smile. He raised his eyebrows, expectantly. Norbert stopped in his tracks and stared at the old man in disbelief.

"Dad?"

From the Author

This is James, the author of Puzzle Forest. I really hope you enjoyed it!

If you (or the person who bought this for you) could review it on Amazon, that would mean the world to me. I love hearing from readers.

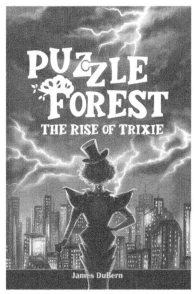

Puzzle Forest 2 - Available now!

The next book in the series is called The Rise of Trixie, and it's a belter! So many questions are answered.

Great big thanks to Kateryna Kirdoglio for the cover, and to my talented editor, Madeleine Rafel. To Lily, for helping shape this story, and to Sophia for your unwavering support.

Finally, thanks to my wonderful wife Jo, for everything.

Made in the USA
Monee, IL
15 April 2025

15870536R00121